THREE CHRISTMAS PRESENTS

and other short stories

Harriet Loveday

Harriet Loveday Romance

Thank you, Theresa and Gill, for your continued support and all the women who have supported me.

CONTENTS

PREFACE

The title story 'Three Christmas Presents' is loosely based on A Christmas Carol. I like the normality of the supernatural in Dickens's work, I like the message of goodness and charity (charity can also be translated from the Greek word agape as love), and I like the idea that we're all redeemable. We all get a second chance if our heart is truly in it.

In 'Three Christmas Presents', the title story, Fiona meets her three ghosts of Christmas: present (death of love), past (uncharitable behaviour) and future (righting her wrongs), and it is only by showing *agape* that she can unlock her future and access her second chance.

I have made so many mistakes in my relationships that I hope, in these stories, you can sympathise with the themes I've brought forward and, as I am ever the romantic, you will hope with me for the characters to face a future of love as the stories unfold.

True love is rare; it is heart-stoppingly beautiful. In these stories, I gift it to you.

Happy Christmas.

HL x (December 2023)

1. NORTHERN LIGHTS

The children giggled and whispered to each other from behind the thick forest tree trunks and threw snowballs at each other.

'Dare you.' George said.

'Don't do it!' Lily called out in alarm.

'Double dare you.' Joachim replied.

'Okay then.' said George, tightening his scarf around his neck and pulling his bobble hat down a little lower.

'Don't do it.' Lily hissed.

But George ignored her. Leaving the safety of the forest, he walked towards the little house owned by the Heartbroken Hermit. George looked back once or twice, to try and show he wasn't afraid, but his step slowed as he trudged through the snow and got closer to the tiny, ultra-modern, cubist house; white with black-framed, triple-glazed windows. George could be spotted from any of the windows and his bravery faltered as he got nearer.

Twilight was starting to fall, and the children should have been home hours ago. George took one last look back at his friends, and walking up the narrow, cleared path, he stretched his arm out, reached forward and. . .

Knock, knock, knock.

George scarpered as fast as he possibly could, while the snow pulled back at him and impeded his progress. George rushed into the woods. Gathering his friends, they all ran as quickly as they could along the muddy lane back to the village.

Inside the cosy house, the hermit sighed. He completely understood why. Avery knew when he came here, that by trying to be alone, people wouldn't let him because he'd made himself a curio. He shook his head; they were just kids. Curiosity was one of the many traits of being human. Avery patted his mongrel dog, Monet, on the head with his outstretched, sleek, black hand and went back to reading his Kindle.

❉ ❉ ❉

You may think it strange, that someone who's had the sunshine baked into their skin should choose to be in a place so alien and cold. But Avery was where he wanted to be; he wanted to be far away from the woman that broke his heart. The heartbreak hurt so much, that he thought he wouldn't live through it. But he did. And now Avery devoted his precious life to his painting. It was what he lived for. Besides, he had the company of Monet – what more could he want? Avery couldn't deny he was sometimes lonely, he just tried not to think about it too much, because the pain of having your heart broken is much worse.

Avery's skin was dark, dark black, like seventy percent pure cocoa, and his natural scent was just as delicious too. He had dark, wide-set eyes, a broad smile, and beautiful snow-white teeth. As he could please himself, he let his hair grow wild and curly. He usually scooped it back into a bun with multicoloured fabric rags. His laugh, if you were ever lucky enough to hear it, was like a deep rumble of thunder dipped in honey. And his manner was slow, easy and gentle. He wasn't completely out of place in this winter wonderland, in fact, the opposite was true, he was perfectly at home.

Avery didn't mind the children coming to tease him at his home now and again. He was almost glad of it. He loved to hear their laughter as they came to tap on his door and dare each other in the woods. In a strange way, it was human contact (other than selling his art to the dealer in town) and it reminded him of the lighter side of life. But his art and the children, even his dog, Monet, were all distractions really. As he closed himself off, he found it harder to avoid his thoughts. The thing he wanted most in the world was the thing that he feared would kill him: the touch of a loving partner and the companionship of a woman.

Avery was a very talented artist. In the spring and summer, he loved the landscapes and the still-life work he did with flowers, he was also rather good at painting life-like animals. When the winter came, he painted the sparkling, snowy pine forests and magical, icy scenes. Avery sold his work online and to a local dealer. He did well enough to maintain his lifestyle. He was content with his life.

Avery sat at his easel. A half-finished canvas in front of him. His brush swooped and *tap, tap, tapped* as he marked out the dark branches of the fir trees, contrasting against the crisp white snow. He cleaned his brush and sat back with satisfaction as the artwork started to come together. Almost as if it had a life of its own.

Sensing his owner was ready for a break, Monet came up and nuzzled Avery, wanting a walk.

Avery laughed in his deep, honeyed way. 'Okay, old friend. Let's have a break, shall we?'

Monet rushed to the door, ready.

* * *

Avery sat in his favourite chair, by the only window in his tiny living room, reading his Kindle and looking out at the dark, wintry landscape before him, bathed in the light of the moon. At his feet Monet snuffled in his sleep; he was chasing squirrels deep in the woods. The smells. The excitement!

Woof, woof, woof. Monet barked in his sleep.

Laughing, Avery bent down to stroke his head, and momentarily looked out at the view.

The moonlight glowed off the thick, fresh snow.

Little stars shone like glittering diamonds in the navy-velvet midnight sky. Excitedly, Avery leant forward in his chair. He could see a familiar green glow on the horizon. He watched it start to grow and take form, with spiralling tendons reaching out before pulling back. Avery sat up straight; undoubtedly there was going to be a display of the northern lights tonight. It was in moments like these, that he felt like the luckiest man alive.

Avery wanted to be a part of the magical landscape. So, he put on his snow jacket and trousers; his thick, fur-lined boots; thick, padded gloves, and called to Monet to come and join him. Immediately, Monet jumped to Avery's command and came to the door.

They walked out onto the snow plain as the sky started to explode into pinks and greens, blues and purples. Avery held his breath as he looked around him. Monet barked with excitement and ran in circles around his owner. Avery craned his head back as far as it would go, and then allowed himself to fall back onto the snow so that he could experience the full light display.

The snow was soft and cool around him, it supported and encased him, as Avery lay back and watched the magical swirling colours unfold. Monet sat near his feet and woofed. They were so lucky.

✳ ✳ ✳

After a while, Avery started to feel cold, and considered it was about time to go back to his tiny house; he didn't want to catch hypothermia.

Suddenly, from nowhere, it started to rain.

A big splodge of water fell on Avery's snowsuit, and then another. Avery quickly pushed himself up to sitting, and he saw that the splodge was a luminous, fluorescent-green paint on his left leg, and on his right leg, it was a glowing, fuchsia-pink paint. Avery raised his eyebrows and cautiously, using his gloved-finger, he poked the paint.

Monet started barking hysterically as a royal-purple splat of paint landed not far from where he was standing.

Woof, woof, woof.

'I know, friend. This is very odd, isn't it?' Avery replied. Then not far from where Avery's head had been in the snow, a splodge of bright, royal-blue paint landed, neatly filling the hole.

Avery jumped to standing. He stood looking at the luminous green paint on his fingers, rubbing them together and trying to gauge the consistency. He looked at Monet and said, 'It can't be? Surely not?' and raised his eyes to the sky, as Monet woofed in affirmation.

Above their heads, the northern lights had filled most of the sky. Arms and tendrils of luminous-green, dark-green, royal-purple-and-blue, and fuchsia-pink, were twisting and turning, fading and growing, bending, sashaying and dancing across the sky. It was nature at its most extreme.

It was the junction between our familiar earth and the oddities of space. The unknown. It was beautiful.

Avery looked around, but there were no children, no noisy neighbours. The village was four miles away. It was Monet and him. He wished he had a companion with him to discuss this strange event, instead he had to keep it to himself. He wasn't going mad. This was perfectly real.

The artist in him wasn't going to waste this opportunity to try a new medium.

Avery whistled to Monet and started to jog back (as best he could) towards his little house. Monet followed not far behind, narrowly avoiding a few more coloured splodges as they fell.

Hurriedly entering his tiny home, Avery rushed to the sink and grabbed some jam jars which were drying on the draining board. He then rushed back outside, holding out the jam jars as he ran and trying to catch the drips as they fell.

✻ ✻ ✻

Avery collected six colours in total. A pearlescent, almost luminous, white; a light, fluorescent-green and a darker, shimmering, fluorescent-green; a deep, royal-purple; a royal-blue, and a bright, fuchsia-pink. He lined them up on his prep table and stared at them in the full light of day. Even in the clear, strong, light of day, the liquid lights glowed.

Fascinated, Avery picked up the jars and watched the contents move as he tried to judge their consistency. Then, Avery did what any artist would do. He cleaned his brushes, took out a new canvas, and carefully studying the collection of colours in front of him, he selected a few and started to paint. He decided to paint some of the forest flowers that grew nearby in the spring, and quickly got about his work.

The paint was malleable and took to the canvas well. Avery's composition came together easily as the still-life of pink and purple flowers amongst the green, spring grass almost looked as if they were growing. Avery felt as if he could just pick them off the page.

Wiping his brow, Avery popped the brushes back into the water and swished them around to clean them. Then wiping his hands on his apron, after a morning's hard work, he stood up to go out to the kitchen. Monet, ever faithful, was hovering at his heels. They left the house to have a walk together in the crisp, bright day and shared lunch together. After lunch, Avery returned to his studio area and couldn't help but stare at his picture.

Avery felt like his picture was growing and moving. The flowers were so realistic it was as if they were alive. Without really thinking about what he was doing, Avery reached out his hand as if he were about to pick one of the little forest flowers. And to his surprise, his hand returned with a tiny little flower, picked between his thumb and forefinger. His painting was alive.

* * *

It wasn't as if Avery could talk about this with anyone. It was very strange, but Avery had also seen many strange things in his life that he didn't understand, so he just went with it. He also did what any artist would do when gifted the most extraordinary paints ever known. He painted.

More flowers, beautiful butterflies, all sorts of wildlife; until he had rabbits jumping out of his doors, and butterflies beating their wings at his windows. Avery considered for half a moment that he could try and sell his artwork. The problem was; people were so greedy. They wanted to consume everything. Avery and his paints, the beautiful liquid lights, would be consumed under a bulldozer of consumption. Yes, he would make money, but he would destroy something so delicate and beautiful that the meaning would be meaningless. No. This was his secret, it was just for him, it was his little piece of winter magic.

Avery's tiny, cubist home was filling up with pots of wilting wildflowers and butterflies crying to be let out to perish in the winter storms. He needed to be more circumspect, he needed to think about what he was painting for. Avery, as with all humans, was a protector of the earth, not a destroyer.

Avery wished he had someone he could talk about this with. It was at times like these he missed human company. Monet nuzzled into Avery's legs as he sat in his favourite chair. Thinking. Avery reached down and said, 'Thank you, my friend. Yes, I do always have you.' Monet licked Avery's hand happily in reply.

Avery let his eyes wander to the dark night outside. A million stars twinkling in the sky. His thoughts wandered far away. Musing on these magical, liquid lights and their enchanted properties.

Avery thought: "I've been able to paint animals and plants. I wonder if I could paint a human?"

❊ ❊ ❊

Once the idea had popped into his head, Avery couldn't shake it. He was so afraid of the thought, that he stopped painting with the liquid lights and went back to his normal acrylics and watercolours.

But the temptation was too great.

If Avery was going to do this, he had to think about it very carefully. Questions whizzed into his head. How would Avery paint her? What sort of person would she be? Her skin would be multicoloured, but it wasn't as if his skin was the native colour of this arctic landscape. She might not be suited to the cold, but he had spare, warm clothes to keep her cosy.

All the animals and flowers Avery had painted were fully functioning. The butterflies had flapped and the bunnies bounced. They were alive, they could breathe, eat and move. A fox had even barked at him before rushing out the door. In all likelihood, she would be able to talk, just like him. If he painted a human female, she would probably be human in almost every way. The one thing that stayed Avery's hand from picking up his brush without delay was the question: Was he playing at being God?

* * *

Avery was frustrated. He shook his head. His artwork wasn't going well at all. He tried not to look at the liquid lights, he knew what would happen.

Then, on one particularly long, dark night, when the children hadn't "called" on him for at least a month, and his art dealer was fully stocked, and Avery was feeling particularly lonely, he found himself thinking incessantly of the liquid lights and painting *her*.

Slowly, Avery got up from his chair. Monet raised his head from his sleeping place at Avery's feet, to watch his master with a worried look.

Avery slowly walked over to his studio and flicked on the light.

He knew exactly what he wanted.

She would have to have a large heart. Be kind and generous. It was going to take all his skill as an artist. If he was going to paint his life partner then he could paint her body exactly as he wanted. Bottoms. He loved curvy bottoms. And beautiful, voluptuous hair. A big wide smile, and sparkling eyes that he could gaze into for hours, and study to catch her feelings. He craved the emotional connection of a woman's eyes.

Avery focussed completely on his vision. He could almost see her forming before his eyes. Excitedly he selected his brushes, got some clean water for his jam jar, and with a shaking hand, brought the liquid lights down from the window-sill.

Avery started to paint.

❊ ❊ ❊

George, Joachim and Lily hid in the woods, looking over to the Heartbroken Hermit's house.

'Dare you.' said Joachim.

'Double dare you.' said George.

Lily wrung her hands with concern. 'Oh no, please don't do it, please don't. Just leave him alone, let's go back and find pinecones to paint for the Christmas trees.'

'I'll go.' said George. He bravely stepped out from the forest and walked across the snowy plain, towards the house, just as the light was starting to fall. Joachim and Lily watched him with wide eyes. His steps started to slow as he got nearer and nearer the tiny house, then, rather than approach the door, they saw him sneak up to one of the windows and peek his head over the window ledge to look in. Not long afterwards he turned around and slowly sneaked back across the snowy plain. The evening light fading all around them.

Joachim and Lily were beside themselves with excitement and fear. 'What did you see?' asked Joachim.

George shook his head. His eyes were wide with surprise. He said, 'You'll never believe it, but I think the Heartbroken Hermit has got a girlfriend.'

George and Joachim looked at each other and started giggling. Lilly held her hands clasped to her heart and said, 'Oh! That's so sweet.'

Joachim said, 'I want to have a look.'

Usually, Lily would have resisted and ask them not to go, but the thought of the poor heartbroken man finally having found love was too much to resist. So, with trepidation, she followed in the footsteps of the two boys as they sneaked across the snow-covered plain towards the hermit's tiny house.

George and Joachim were already at the window, just peeking their heads above the ledge and looking into the warmly lit, tiny, living room. Lily joined them, and shaking with fear, she too raised her head just enough to see inside.

There were two chairs sat side by side in the tiny living room. In one the hermit had a Kindle on his lap and he was reading out loud. In the other seat sat the most extraordinary-coloured woman. She was smiling and listening to him. Her hair was the colour of unicorns; her eyes were a luminous, deep violet; her skin was pale and iridescent almost like the snow. She wore a loose tracksuit and had a furry blanket over her lap. The hermit's dog was sat beside her, and she was stroking the dog's head as they all listened to the hermit reading.

She was so bewitching, the children could hardly take their eyes off her.

The Heartbroken Hermit stopped reading. He set his Kindle gently on the small table stand, got up, leant forward, and kissed the remarkable lady on the forehead, before wandering through to his tiny kitchen.

All three children ducked below the window ledge and looking at each other with eyes as big as the creamy moon, they ran away giggling.

It seemed the Heartbroken Hermit wasn't so lonely anymore.

2. THREE CHRISTMAS PRESENTS

'Stacey!' Colin Pritchard hollered for his personal assistant through the open glass door.

Nonplussed, Stacey, a slim, efficient brunette, saved what she was working on, gracefully got up from her swivel chair, and grabbed a notepad, pen and her phone as she walked through to Colin's big office.

Colin looked up, irritated. 'Close the door, Stacey.' His short brown hair was starting to grey at the temples, and the lines and wrinkles on his face were getting deeper with each stressful year, even the suntan from his holidays didn't really cover the wrinkles anymore. Colin had brown eyes and a pointed nose, his eyebrows were thick and expressive, and he was just short of six feet tall, something that always irked him.

Stacey knew that this must be about his personal life, because the closed door either meant personal life or secret business deals, and irritability plus a closed door definitely meant personal life.

Stacey entered the room and sat down opposite her boss, Colin. She had a good idea what this was going to be about.

The office Christmas cookie drop had clearly made it to Colin's desk. Stacey thought, "You can't keep a figure, if you're eating sugar." Stacey pursed her lips and prepared for the meeting with her phone notes open: she couldn't have any evidence once the task was complete.

Clearing his throat, Colin said, 'I know that you understand this is very delicate, and just between us.' Stacey nodded efficiently. This was no different to the last two years, although the year before that one of the women had been different.

Stacey replied, 'Of course, absolute confidentiality.'

Colin continued, 'I like things in threes,' Colin said enigmatically, 'so three presents each.' Stacey wondered if he liked his women in threes too. If so, who was the other woman? Her? Colin continued, 'To be clear that's three Christmas presents for the missus, and three for my girlfriend. First of all: get my girlfriend something silky, I think she's a size twelve; some expensive perfume, I can't remember the exact one she likes so anything will do, just leave the purchase receipt inside the box so if she doesn't like it, she can take it back; and finally, some of those nice expensive champagne truffles from Fortnum and Mason. Oh, and get yourself some truffles as well for the trouble, but not more than thirty pounds though.'

Stacey nodded, her fingers typing rapidly. 'Thank you. And what about your wife? What do you want me to buy her?'

Colin ran his fingers over his lips. '*Humm*. Yes, right. She's in the kitchen a lot, so something for the kitchen. Wooden spoons? Cookbooks? Err a food voucher. Yes, a food voucher for somewhere, some wooden spoons, and let's say an apron. That'll be great. Try not to spend more than a hundred on her and make it look like it's three times the price.'

'Yes, of course, Colin.' Stacey tapped away efficiently. The problem was, things tended to look like their price, you can't make things look three times the price. If you're not willing to spend very much, then it doesn't look like very much. Stacey looked up at her boss and gave a tight smile, 'And the budget for the girlfriend?'

'Oh yes. Right. Five hundred, because she'll know. Actually, scrap the truffles and I'll give her a weekend away somewhere, only make sure it's covered as a business trip in my calendar. Don't want the wife to know.'

Stacey didn't flinch as she asked, 'And the budget for that, Colin?' Stacey tapped away efficiently deleting the truffles. She was glad, Fortnum and Mason would be heaving at this time of year.

Colin tried to do calculations in his head, 'Err, no more than five hundred again on the weekend away if you can get away with it.'

Stacey nodded, 'Noted. Do you want me to start this now?'

Colin dismissed her from his office with a swish of his hand, 'Yes, start now. And can you get them wrapped as well? I don't do wrapping.'

'Absolutely. Happy Christmas.'

'Yes. Ho ho ho and all that.' Colin didn't even bother to look up as Stacey left the room.

* * *

The truth was, Stacey had been offered a personal assistant position for the chief financial officer. This was the last year that she had to put up with this. Leaving the office, she decided she would go to Fortnum and Mason after all. She found some gold-dusted champagne truffles for her troubles and purchased them on Colin's business account. After exiting the shop, she immediately opened the box and popped one into her mouth. These errands were going to take her all afternoon and the city was packed with people, she was going to need these little treats to keep her going. Stacey felt a little sad. It was his wife she felt sorry for. She really had no idea. It seemed like Stacey was supposed to get assorted kitchen goods for his wife and luxurious, exciting presents for his girlfriend. It didn't seem fair. How can you give someone wooden kitchen spoons for Christmas? Stacey had spoken to Colin's wife, Fiona, on the phone several times, and she knew she liked shabby-chic décor. There was a little antiques shop around the corner. Stacey decided she'd go there and have a look.

It was almost like stepping back into a time warp, stepping into the old antiques shop. A small, brass doorbell pinged Stacey's arrival as she entered. All around her were antiques; old clocks, side tables, faded paintings, curios. All piled up on top of each other in precarious towers that looked as if they were about to fall at any moment. An old man, with wispy white hair; half-moon glasses; wearing a faded-blue smoking jacket; and red, velvet fez with a black tassel perched on his head, greeted her.

The antiques dealer said, 'Merry Christmas, my dear. Are you looking for anything in particular?'

Stacey shook her head, 'I don't know yet. It's for a female friend. She's into shabby-chic décor, but also items of quality. I just came in here for inspiration.' Stacey offered the old man a gold-dusted truffle, which he inspected, then smilingly accepted.

Sucking the truffle, he looked thoughtful. 'Ah!' the old man held his index finger in the air as if he'd just had the perfect idea or heard the perfect words. 'I know exactly the thing that might suit her. A Victorian, cut-glass, ornate mirror. Come with me.' The old man dashed in between piles of furniture and old paintings, as he led Stacey through the labyrinth of antiques, to the back of the shop.

The mirror was right at the back of the shop, hung on the wall. It was about the size of a silver serving tray, and oval in shape; with delicate cut glass patterns along the edges; it had scrollwork at the top and the bottom; and the mirror behind the glass was mottled and blackened in places where it was flaking with age, giving the mirror an authentic antique look.

'You know,' Stacey said, 'I think this is exactly what I was looking for.'

The old man almost winked at the efficient personal assistant. Nodding, he affirmed, 'I thought it might be.'

Stacey turned to the old man, 'I need it packaged carefully, so it won't break, and I need it sent to my office by the end of the day.'

'I will have one of the boys make a box for it immediately, and have it sent round to your office by four p.m. Will that suit?' The old man was confident of his sale.

Stacey nodded. 'Yes, that will suit perfectly.'

The personal assistant and the antiques dealer shook on it.

❋ ❋ ❋

Fiona idly flipped the pages of the home magazine, in her enormous orangery-style conservatory. Raising her eyes from her magazine, she looked out the back of the house, to the perfectly manicured lawn, and sighed with boredom. Her champagne-blonde curls fell in a modern shaggy bob to her shoulders, and her light-grey eyes continued to stare sadly out at the garden. Fiona had a slim, oval face, neat features, and clear skin; helped by her little cosmetic pick-me-ups.

Colin didn't want children yet, he said. Fiona longed for children. She loved children, but she also loved her luxurious lifestyle. She loved the ease of buying whatever she wanted, whenever she wanted. The question was, did she love children more? She didn't know, and the more she pondered the thought, the more time seemed to slip by. Another year, another Christmas. Colin always told her, how fond he was of her, and she was very fond of him too. Their life was very pleasant together, except that he worked so hard, and he was rarely home. But when he was home, they enjoyed each other's company. Fiona felt a little sad that he didn't take a romantic interest in her anymore, but she guessed it was just the way marriage went, wasn't it? Wasn't it like that, as couples grow old together? She was going to be thirty-eight years old on her next birthday. Fiona knew that they were leaving it late for children, but she also thought that she wouldn't be able to find anyone else now anyway. If she asked him again this Christmas, then maybe he'd agree this time.

Fiona looked at her phone. It was empty. Colin didn't message her much anymore. She'd call him at the office, but she knew he was always busy, and he'd just be annoyed talking to her. Besides, he was working hard to provide a beautiful home and life for them; their lovely holidays; the great parties with all their friends. Fiona lived a good life.

Sighing deeply, Fiona tucked her champagne-blonde curls back behind her ear, turning her attention back to yet another home magazine. Perhaps she should re-decorate the lounge next year?

* * *

Fiona was quite surprised when Colin came home just before Christmas with three-unusual looking Christmas presents for her. The boxes were all wrapped in dark-green paper with large pink bows. She didn't know he had it in him, although the last three years he had put a lot of thought into his gifts. She almost felt excited at the thought of opening them. One present was a large rectangular box, it was very heavy. She placed it at the bottom of the pile of presents under the Christmas tree. The second present was a smaller rectangular box, and very light. Fiona almost wanted to give it a shake, thinking it could give a clue as to what was inside, but she didn't want to break it, so she just placed it carefully amongst the pile of presents under the tree. The third box was very small, about the size of an envelope. Fiona hoped it might be jewellery; she always loved to receive jewellery.

Colin and Fiona had thrown the usual rounds of pre-Christmas parties at their house, including a drinks evening for some of the other managers at his work and particularly the managers above him that he wanted to impress. Fiona even got to meet his personal assistant, Stacey, this year.

Colin had never invited Stacey before, but it appeared that Stacey was going to be leaving him to be the personal assistant for the chief financial officer. Colin saw his drinks evening as an opportunity to flatter Stacey before she left.

Fiona had wondered if Colin had been having an affair with Stacey, but when she met her, she realised instantly this couldn't be the case, because Stacey and Colin appeared to interact on a plane of mutual efficiency and tolerance, the chemistry between them was like watching two pieces of deadwood bashing against each other as they sped along a river in flood.

It was silly, Fiona didn't know why she'd thought he was having an affair, Colin was married to his work.

When it came to Christmas Eve, Fiona always insisted on her granny's treat to her when she was a little girl; she was always allowed to open one Christmas present from under the tree. Colin didn't mind particularly, but just as Fiona was choosing her present from under the tree, he had an urgent work phone call, and excused himself to go to his study.

Fiona was used to it, she didn't bother waiting because she knew that he could be a while, so instead she sat alone in the lounge and picked out a present that she wanted to open.

Fiona picked the second present; the small rectangular box that was quite light. She hoped it was something exciting.

Like a little girl, she pulled off the pink ribbon and lifted the lid off the green box, to reveal the most exquisite, black, silk-and-lace lingerie. There was a night dress, a dressing gown and a little camisole and knicker set. Fiona touched the soft fabric and checked the label. It was the perfect size! Little tears welled in Fiona's eyes. She'd thought that Colin had forgotten about the physical side of their relationship, she'd almost started to wonder if he found her attractive at all anymore. Clearly, this was his way of telling her that he still loved her, and he still wanted her.

Fiona tried to choke back the tears that were welling up inside her. He did notice her after all. Taking a deep breath, she decided she knew the best way to show him that she completely understood what he was trying to tell her with this gift; that he still listened, he still heard her and that perhaps they should try for children. Fiona knew what to do.

Grabbing the box, and eagerly rushing upstairs, Fiona quickly changed into the camisole and knickers. She slipped the cool, thick, black silk robe over her. Tying the belt and arranging the lace on the lapel, she delicately tiptoed downstairs. If Colin could make a grand gesture, then she could too. She decided that she would do something seductively crazy, something she never did.

Hesitantly, Fiona opened Colin's study door ajar, and peeked her leg around the door to see if he noticed. Inside she could hear he was on the phone. Fiona smiled, maybe this would tempt him to put business aside for five minutes and focus on her?

Colin continued talking on his phone. His voice

was an urgent whisper. He appeared completely engrossed in the call. Curiously, Fiona peeked her head around the door to find that he had his back to her. He was leant forward over his desk. He seemed to be talking in a loud whisper trying to mollify someone. He almost looked like he was panting.

Fiona dropped her leg and stood there stupefied, as she heard little bits of his conversation:

. . . 'Darling, I don't think you are a cook, I'm not asking you to cook for me. I'd never do that. There must have been some mix-up.' He stood hunched over his desk, cradling the phone and pleading with the caller. There was a long pause. Then, Colin made an almost growl as he said, 'You don't understand how much I want you. How much I've been imagining ripping that black silk off your body. I don't know what happened. I'll get you another set. . . Yes, two other sets. A red one too. I promise. I'll make up for this, I promise.' Colin's body was propped up by his right hand leaning on his desk, his body crunched further over his phone, his breathing came in hard gasps. Colin wasn't even aware that Fiona was there.

Fiona stood there. As still as a statue. It didn't matter if he saw her or not. Colin wasn't interested in being aware that Fiona heard, he wasn't aware of anything in the room right now other than the woman that he was talking to on the phone, and their conversation which appeared to revolve around sex. Yet, Fiona was supposed to be his wife.

It seemed that the lingerie she was wearing was destined for another woman, and she was to have received some cooking utensils. That's the reality of how he saw her.

Fiona swallowed as if she'd eaten a whole hardboiled egg. She felt empty and cold. Lonely and sad. All at the same time. Her life was a sham. She was worthless. Fiona looked around at the cleverly fabricated lie she lived in. But what was worse, was that she almost felt as if she'd known that her world was an empty shell for a long time now, and she'd been compliant in the lie; she'd been willing to be a part of it.

Slowly and sadly, Fiona turned around and gently closed the study door behind her. She padded upstairs, and replaced the beautiful black lingerie into the green box and retied the pink ribbon. It wasn't her gift.

The reality of now hit Fiona full force. In her imagined reality she was living in a beautiful house with children and a loving husband, everything was clean and easy. Fiona realised that the other woman on the phone was her actual Christmas present, the gift was to know what truly exists. Her present was to fully understand that her reality was a hollow sham. A lie. The ghost of her imagined reality; a laughing, carefree mother, slipped away.

Fiona was angry at herself for creating a life that didn't exist, and to acknowledge that perhaps she'd had her suspicions for a while. She'd known for a long time their marriage wasn't working, but she'd been too comfortable with their luxurious lifestyle to do anything about it. She'd been willing to turn a blind eye to a husband that didn't love her, so that she could live in material excess. Perhaps the hurt she was feeling, she'd brought upon herself.

Fiona washed and put on her pyjamas. She slowly crawled into bed. The sheets were cool, and she turned off the lamp, lying there, motionless.

Fiona lay still and awake for at least another two hours before Colin came to bed. How much of that time he'd spent talking to his mistress on the phone, she didn't know. Fiona closed her eyes and pretended that she was asleep so that she didn't have to talk to him. When he started snoring, she let the cold tears flow, and lay there, silently, on her wet pillow.

* * *

Fiona was at a complete loss for what to do. She hadn't confronted Colin, and she didn't really know how to. So, she just tried to carry on.

The next day, Christmas Day, his parents came around for Christmas lunch. And following tradition, just after the King's speech, they opened the presents underneath the Christmas tree, while drinking glasses of champagne.

Fiona had a feeling of dread as she looked at the other two presents. She wasn't sure she wanted to open them. With trepidation, she undid the pink bow and slid back the green paper on the large, rectangular, heavy box. She was pleasantly surprised to find a cut-glass, old, ornate, Victorian mirror. For half a moment, Fiona wondered if this had been destined for the other woman too, but Colin said confidently, 'Darling, I know you love these sorts of things, and I hope this is the right style for the house? I thought it could replace the one you didn't like in the hall?'

Colin's parents exchanged sweet, loving glances at their happily married son and daughter-in-law, and Fiona appropriately said, 'Absolutely! It's perfect. I know just where you mean.'

Going out to the hall, Colin helped Fiona to take down the modern, square mirror hung over the hall table, and replaced it with this beautiful Victorian antique instead.

Fiona stood gazing at the mirror. 'It's beautiful.' she said to him, a little tear in her eye.

Colin squeezed her shoulder and said, 'I'm glad you like it darling. I thought you would.' He grabbed his champagne and went back to the lounge where his parents were sat opening their presents.

Fiona stood for a moment in front of the mirror. It reminded her of a very similar mirror that used to hang in her grandmother's bedroom.

Suddenly, her granny was facing her in the mirror. The same oval face as her but with wrinkles and jowls, the same tired, light-grey eyes. Her grey hair was scraped back. She looked cross and said to Fiona, 'I did tell you, my dear: you lose them how you get them. Don't look for sympathy from me, young lady.'

Fiona placed her hand over her mouth in shock. But the only person staring back at her in the mirror was herself. She shivered and averted her eyes. Looking back in the mirror she saw herself as a sad middle-aged lady, stood in a luxurious home.

The hard truth her granny had delivered was correct. Fiona had cheated when she'd met Colin.

✳ ✳ ✳

Fiona had met Colin when she was eighteen, working in a fast-food restaurant, flipping burgers. Colin was a local hotshot, who'd given up his school studies to work as a manager at the local supermarket. He'd even bought himself a flashy, second-hand car. Fiona had been impressed by his obvious displays of wealth. The problem was, Fiona already had a boyfriend and Colin had a girlfriend.

Ben.

Fiona's heart twisted as she thought back to him. Lovely, Ben. She even felt tingly thinking about him now, after all these years. She was stupid when she was eighteen, she didn't realise that love is rare, it's not common, you don't find it around every street corner, you're lucky if it comes to you once in your life.

Ben had worked at the fast-food restaurant with her. He was kind and warm and he adored her. They loved their time together. Being around Ben was magical; he had an easy nature, and his sunny brown eyes matched his warm brown hair and honey-tanned skin. Ben always kept himself physically fit; he'd run for miles; cycle to work every day; he'd play golf with his granddad, and he was very good, but he didn't want to be a golfer. He didn't seem to want to go anywhere or do anything.

Colin had come into the fast-food restaurant and sized up Fiona as an acquisition to add to his pile of stuff, to show how successful he was. She was to be yet another trophy in the line of things that he collected as he proclaimed to the world: "Look at who I am!" He didn't love her, and if she was honest, she didn't love him. But at the time, she'd thought she did. She'd been young and stupid. Colin had showered her with a lot of attention, and he had money. He seemed like a better bet than Ben.

Fiona had done the unthinkable. She'd flirted with Colin and split him up from his girlfriend, then she left Ben, broken-hearted and crying. Fiona had turned her back and walked away.

Looking around, Fiona saw she'd got what she wanted. A big house, a luxurious lifestyle, and a man that treated her like a possession. Fiona should have realised it would come to this, as Colin was showing her as much regard as his previous girlfriend before her. Fiona and Colin had both cheated on their partners when they'd got together, and now Colin was cheating on her.

Her granny was right. You lose them how you get them.

Colin broke Fiona's thoughts. 'Darling! Darling! We've opened all our presents, there is only one present left.'

Fiona felt nervous as she turned to face the lounge and walked in, wondering what ghost this third present was going to deliver her.

❊ ❊ ❊

Later that day, before dinner, Colin's dad, Fiona's father-in-law, made a joke about Fiona's slightly burnt beef Wellington saying, 'Well, you can always use that voucher, and get one of those delivery people to bring some food out if this doesn't work.' Fiona's mother-in-law gave him a nudge and shushed him, but smiled slightly at the edge of her mouth at the catty remark.

Fiona tried to be congenial and laugh. She wiped her brow from the heat of the kitchen. She wasn't a cook, in fact, her cook usually left everything ready for her to reheat, which was why the beef Wellington was slightly burnt, because she wasn't used to using the oven.

They were quite right though, the third present, her meal delivery voucher, could be used in an emergency. It was a bit strange, to receive an eat-in meal voucher for two. If Fiona didn't know about the other woman, she might have thought that Colin was suggesting a romantic night in for the two of them, now she just wondered if her cooking was so bad, he thought he'd use a Christmas present as a "phone a friend" to ensure he got a decent meal. The silly thing was, they had a housekeeper, they didn't need to order in meals.

Externally, Fiona was cheerful and smiley, internally she was cold and numb, just trying to work her way through the days. Christmas Day evening, as they were climbing into bed, Colin announced that there had been some kind of emergency at work, and he was going to leave tomorrow morning to go into the city and sort it. Fiona nodded and said she understood.

Fiona thought back to all the times that she'd heard this excuse before, and she wondered how often it was true and how often he was going to see his mistress. Fiona couldn't trust anything he said anymore. She wasn't sure she could even trust herself.

* * *

Fiona filled the days between Christmas and New Year by seeing friends and playing with their children. Her mind was a whirr as she questioned her future and thought back to the life choices she'd made. Fiona realised that at eighteen she'd behaved in a selfish and cruel way, and she'd got exactly what she deserved. A beautiful, empty, lonely house, and a life without children or love. If she had her chance to do it all over again, would she choose differently?

＊ ＊ ＊

It was the morning of New Year's Eve. Fiona had got up early. She'd completed her half an hour run on her treadmill, had a shower and went downstairs to eat her overnight-soaked oats with nuts and berries. Colin stayed in bed, but by the time he entered the kitchen, he was dressed in a work shirt paired with smart trousers. Fiona knew what he was going to say before he said it.

'Darling, I'm so sorry to tell you this, I need to go back in to work this morning. I'm not sure how late I'll be. But we were only going to have a quiet night tonight, just us, weren't we? So, it won't matter if I'm late. Start the champagne without me, and *hopefully* I'll be back before midnight.' Then Judas kissed her on the forehead, grabbed his briefcase, and was gone. Fiona couldn't remember if she'd given him a reply, she wasn't sure that he'd be interested in listening anyway.

Fiona looked out of the back of her large orangery-style conservatory. She looked out over her perfectly manicured lawn, decorated with a tasteful assortment of fairy-lit reindeer, who were pretending to eat the grass. She stared at the reindeer models and tried to focus on what she wanted for her future.

Now that Fiona knew about Colin's mistress, and she could see through his lies, was she willing to continue like this? Just so that she could enjoy this luxurious, easy life? She had to accept that Colin would never want children – he'd been stringing her along as she aged.

Fiona wondered what it would be like to be poor again. . . In her mind, she was back to flipping burgers at eighteen years old, with Ben, in the kitchen at the fast-food restaurant. They were throwing baps at each other and laughing. She could see him clearly, dancing as he cooked. His muscly legs protruding from his apron. He was suggesting crazy ideas for things that they could do over the weekend. Her thoughts were broken by his crumpled face when she broke his heart and told him that she didn't want to be his girlfriend anymore.

Fiona shook her head, and her champagne-blonde waves swished either side of her oval face as she tried to clear her head of her thoughts. Fiona didn't want to think what her life would be like now if she'd chosen differently. She didn't want to know what an alternative life with Ben would have looked like.

On the quartzite kitchen island worktop, alongside her BMW keys, and her platinum credit card, sat the gourmet meal eat-in vouchers. If Colin wasn't going to be here, then what was the point in cooking? She might as well blow her last present. Did it matter if it was a meal for two? If she ordered it now, she could order herself a banquet; she could choose all the different meals that she liked. She didn't have to eat it all, she could just have a bit of fun, open a bottle of champagne, and watch rom-coms. In contrast to the week Fiona had had, the prospect almost seemed pleasant.

Fiona's thoughts were broken by the ringing of the telephone in the hall. Leaving her breakfast half-eaten, Fiona went out to the hall and cautiously picked up the phone. There had been so many shocks the last week, she didn't know what to expect anymore.

A polite and efficient-sounding lady spoke out to her, 'Hello? Hello? Is that Mrs Pritchard?'

Slightly shakily, Fiona replied, 'Yes, who's speaking?'

The polite lady continued, 'Oh that's wonderful. I'm calling from Enchanted Escapes Hotels about the booking your husband made? We're ever so sorry but there appears that there's been a bit of a mix-up with the booking. I believe one of our representatives told you that we weren't able to book the nights of the 1 and 2 January this week, and I know your husband was upset because it's your birthday, but there's been a cancellation, and if you still want the booking rather than the weekend in March, then we can accommodate you. We're terribly sorry for the confusion over this and for contacting you at late notice.'

Fiona could barely move. Her birthday was in June. How many more deceptions were going to come pouring out? How long could she keep this up for? Why had she never seen this before? Why was this happening to her now?

The lady on the phone said, 'Hello? Hello? Are you still there Mrs Pritchard?'

'Yes, I'm here.' Fiona called out brightly. She didn't care anymore; it was his silly money and his silly mistress. Fiona answered, 'That's great news, yes, we'll be there for the 1 and 2 January. Thank you so much for contacting us.'

The lady continued, 'I can see that the rooms have both been paid for up-front as part of the all-inclusive package with meals and drinks included, let me resend the booking details to you now to confirm the booking. Can I confirm your e-mail address?'

Fiona sighed. What was she to do? Tell the lady that actually this was a dirty little two nights away for her husband and his mistress? Perhaps she could use it as her exposé piece to tell him that she knew? Perhaps she could just let the details come to her and watch him squirm as he tried to work his way out of this one? Absentmindedly, Fiona said, 'Yes, sure, my e-mail address is. . .'

* * *

It was seven-thirty p.m. on New Year's Eve, and Fiona was alone in the house, waiting for her gourmet food delivery to arrive. She'd ordered: scallops with parsley and buckwheat; oysters with pickled green apple; duck with roasted plantains and purple broccoli in a parsley yoghurt; halibut with courgettes, a green bean vinaigrette and a Brazil nut cream. To finish there was a chocolate tart and a passion fruit and mango pavlova. Fiona was going to see the New Year in, in style.

Selecting a particularly expensive champagne from Colin's wine cellar (from his in-built, precision temperature, wine fridges) Fiona poured herself a flute of champagne, toasted herself and said, 'Fiona, this is the point where you decide what direction you're going to take in life. Do you stay here, in this beautiful house, in a loveless relationship, feeling cold and empty? Or do you take a leap and choose a different life, no matter how scary that may be?'

Fiona didn't have an answer for herself, but she did take a good glug of champagne, and she felt an awful lot better. Listening to Christmas music, sipping her champagne, and scrolling her phone, Fiona sat patiently at the kitchen island, waiting for her delicious dinner to arrive.

Not more than five minutes later there was a ring at the front door. Considering it was New Year's Eve the timing was impressive. Fiona went into the hall. She placed her champagne flute on the side table, looked into the beautiful Victorian mirror, and remembering her granny's words, Fiona tried not to be too hard on herself, she took a deep breath and opened the front door.

'Ben!' Fiona stood there, stupefied.

In front of her stood Ben, holding her food

order. The same warm, sunny, cheerful personality, only twenty years older. It was like she'd seen a ghost. His face was wrinkled and tired, but he still had the same, brown-coloured, happy eyes. Except when he saw Fiona. She watched as lightning bolts of pain jetted across his face; his mouth twisted and he looked away.

Fiona repeated herself in shock and surprise, 'Ben. It's me. It's me, Fiona.'

Ben clearly knew who she was, he just didn't want to talk to her. Clearing his throat and getting back to business he said, 'Hi Fiona. It's good to see you after all these years. I hope you're keeping well? I have your food order.'

Fiona still stood at the door as she exclaimed, 'I didn't know that you still did food?'

Ben shifted the weight of the box in his arms as he replied, 'Yes, I run the company now, no other sucker is going to be out on New Year's Eve, right? You're my last cover today.' Ben looked down at the large box in his hands and looking back up at her said, 'I can drop this in your kitchen if you like?'

Fiona held the door open for him, 'Yes, please do come on through.' She pulled the door back a little wider, and carefully shut it behind him. She then followed him, her eyes wide in amazement, through to her kitchen.

Ben looked around uncomfortably. Conversationally, he said, 'Nice place you have here.' He wiped his sweating hands on his jeans.

Bluntly, Fiona replied, 'Yeah, it's nice, and lonely,

and cold.'

Ben looked strangely at Fiona, but tried to remain professional as he opened the boxes. Ben started to explain the last-minute preparations needed so that her meal would be perfect. Then he knitted his eyebrows together and looked at her, 'But you've ordered for two?'

Again, Fiona bluntly replied, 'Yes, that's right. My husband is with his mistress tonight. He's bought her some new lingerie, so he won't be home. I thought I'd treat myself.' Even Fiona was slightly shocked at what was coming out of her mouth, but she couldn't help herself, it was almost as if during the last week the words had been pent up and brewing within her, and now she finally had a friend and confidant, she let it all out.

Ben tried to hold on to his last ounce of professionalism. He cleared his throat and said, 'Well, yes. Okay, so I hope you enjoy your meal. And Happy New Year.'

Fiona reached over and touched Ben on the arm saying, 'Did you say I was your last cover?'

Ben shifted uncomfortably on his feet, 'Yes.'

Without thinking or considering that he might have a girlfriend, Fiona said, 'Would you like to share this meal with me?'

As luck would have it, Ben had broken up with his girlfriend just three months ago. One of a long line of girlfriends, because no one compared to the girl that got away, Fiona. Ben had longed for her, pined for her, and now here she was, asking him to stay.

But she'd cheated on him and broken his heart. She was married to the man she cheated on him with, and he was stood in that man's house. Ben was angry. He didn't feel comfortable despite what Fiona had said about mistresses. It was starting to sound a little bit complicated to him. But still, he hesitated. Fiona was all he'd ever wanted.

Fiona saw Ben hesitate. She had a good idea why. Reaching out to touch his muscly arm she said, 'It's New Year's Eve and I'm all alone. I've been all alone for a very long time. Please, as friends, please will you stay with me for dinner and to see in the New Year?'

Hesitating, Ben looked down at the warm food in front of him and looked up at Fiona's imploring light-grey eyes and said, 'Okay then.'

* * *

Fiona and Ben dined at the best restaurant in town; Ben's eat-in delivery. They drank champagne, reminisced, and laughed at each other's Christmas cracker hats. Fiona encouraged Ben through to her lounge where, by the light of the fairy lights on the cream-and-white decorated Christmas tree, they watched silly Christmas romcoms together (Ben always was a movie softie). As it neared midnight they turned on the TV to watch Big Ben chime in the New Year. They crossed hands and sang out 'Auld Lang Syne' to each other before collapsing laughing.

Helping Fiona up, Ben continued to hold her hand and said, 'I know you confided a lot to me this evening, and it sounds like last year wasn't much fun, so I hope you have a good year this year, Fiona. Truly I do.'

Fiona looked deep into his warm-brown eyes. In one evening, he'd brought all the joy and sunshine back to her life. She'd laughed so much this evening, her tummy was hurting. It was as if twenty years had melted away in moments, and they were teenagers again, throwing baps at each other, and getting shouted at by their teenage manager in the fast-food restaurant. With all her heart and best wishes, Fiona tried to fix the years of hurt that she'd caused him.

Fiona said, 'Ben, you are one of the best men I've ever met. I've never stopped thinking about you and feeling terrible for the way I'd treated you. With all my heart, I truly wish you a wonderful year, and I honestly hope. . .' Fiona paused, took a gulp, and with a tear in her eye said her truth, '. . . I really hope you find the love you deserve, because you've always deserved someone better than me, and nothing would make me happier than to see you in love.'

Tears sprang to Ben's eyes as he said, 'Never stopped loving you, Fiona. No other girl for me. If I can't have you, then I don't want anyone.'

Boldly, Ben stepped forward and kissed her.

✽ ✽ ✽

Fiona and Ben continued talking into the small hours of the morning. Eventually the good food, good company and fine champagne got the better of them, and they fell asleep on the sofa, wrapped in each other's arms, with a faux fur blanket over them.

Ben was the first to wake the next morning. His eyes were hazy, and he looked around uncertainly until he looked at Fiona. As she came into focus, he said, 'Fiona? Fiona? Is it you?' He looked at her imploringly, as if he'd woken from a dream, into some impossible heaven. Ben could hardly believe his eyes. The events of the day before came back to him, and he smiled contentedly as he looked down at her, wrapped in his arms.

Fiona blinked and slowly opened her eyes. Looking up, she smiled the same contented smile back to him, and said, 'Yes, it's me. Just me. I'm here.'

It was Ben's turn to be blunt. He said, 'I guess today's the day I get to lose you all over again.'

Fiona replied, 'It doesn't have to be. I know I was wrong, I'm so sorry I hurt you. I know I made a mistake. But it's not too late, is it? We could still have a future together, couldn't we?'

Ben looked at her sadly and shook his head. 'You're married Fiona, and I don't take another man's wife. That's not who I am.'

'Oh, that's not a problem.' Fiona said, 'Let me clear that up right away.' She got up and went over to the bureau. Opening it she took out a writing pad and pen. Sitting down she wrote a letter and passed it to Ben, for him to read.

Colin, thank you for our years together. We did as well as we could, considering. I know about your mistress, and I have decided to move on too. By the time you read this letter, I'll be gone. Fiona x

Ben held the letter in amazement, shaking slightly, and looked at her. 'Do you mean it? Would you give up all of this for me? I'm not rich.'

Fiona was never more certain of anything in her life. She said, 'I mean it.'

In amazement, Ben confirmed, 'And you want to come with me? Today? You don't even know where I live.'

Fiona thought for a second, 'Well I guess I might as well go out in style. Yes, I'm happy to move in with you, but I have a different idea for tonight, if that's okay with you?'

❋ ❋ ❋

Ben drove his catering van up the wide drive of the beautiful country house hotel and made a low whistle. 'I guess you might as well make the most of it, because I can't afford hotels like this!'

Fiona fiddled with the cuffs on her cashmere jumper as she said, 'Well the mistress gets spoilt, so if I'm going out on a high, and leaving it all behind, then one last hurrah won't hurt.' She turned to Ben and winked, and they both started laughing.

Ben looked down at the boats on the lake. 'If you have ideas of pushing me off the boat, I'm just telling you now, I'll swim back to shore without you, and you'll have to do your own rowing.'

Fiona shook her head and said, 'I'm like Mariah Carey; I don't do rowing or stairs.'

They both started laughing.

Ben pulled up in front of the enormous country house. The gravel car park crunched under the van tyres. He said with a slight twist to his mouth, 'You know, in a strange sort of way, I'm quite enjoying taking back what was always mine.'

Ben looked over at Fiona, straight into her light-grey eyes. Two souls connected forever.

Fiona said, 'Yes, I've always been yours. I was just too greedy and blind to see it. I hope I can make it up to you.'

Ben shook the sadness away and said, 'Well, I guess we've got two days to have a little bit of fun, haven't we!' Together, they laughed like teenagers excited for their next adventure.

3. SANTA SNOW GLOBE

Tracy was nearing thirty. She surveyed herself in her full-length bedroom mirror and critically appraised why she was still single. Tracy had straight brunette hair; light-blue eyes; a curvy, soft figure; and was slightly below average height. Everybody told her that she really should have a boyfriend, as if she hadn't made an effort. She wanted to shout out: 'It's not as if I'm a dragon with scales.' Instead, in her self-effacing way, she said, 'All the good ones have gone.' Or, 'You know how it is with work, busy, busy.' Or, 'I just don't seem to have any luck with men.'

The last answer was nearer the truth. Tracy had had awful luck. There was the non-committal boyfriend who dumped her as soon as they finished their degrees. Then there was the librarian, who was such a workaholic he seemed to love his books more than her, and in the end, she got fed up with being stood up for a book. Then there was the mummy's boy. Tracy was tired of it, she just wanted someone that wanted her, was that too much to ask? It was even worse now that the Christmas season was drawing near; everyone was having parties and she always seemed to be the odd one out, like an extra gooseberry standing in the corner; or even worse, if there was a male gooseberry around, there was some kind of expectation that she'd partner up with him, no matter how boring or how bad his body-odour was. *Ugh.*

* * *

Tracy decided to cheer herself up and went Christmas shopping in the town where she lived.

In the main part of the town's mediaeval square, they had set up an open-air Christmas market. Little wooden stalls had fake snow over their rooves, and little fairy lights adorned them. There were a few speakers dotted around the square, wafting twinkling background Christmas music over the airwaves, and in the centre of the square, the local church choir was singing Christmas carols.

The most delicious smells drifted over to Tracy. There was a home-baked goods stall, a mulled wine stall and somebody else making non-Christmassy beef burgers and hot dogs, the stall was called "Burgers and Bangers"; delicious just the same.

Everybody seemed happy and in a good mood. Tracy was sure that she would find some perfect presents today and wandered slowly around the stalls. But all the time the question was at the back of her mind: Would love ever happen to her?

Tracy wandered over to a stall. The lady had made lots of different homemade hats. Some were like deerstalkers, others were bobble hats, and some were for children with little animals on top. Tracy bought two animal hats for her nieces. Storing her wares in her jute shopping bag, she thanked the lady and moved on to the next stall.

This stall was selling homemade fudge, and the stallholder kindly gave her a few tasters to try. The orange fudge was delicious, and the rum and raisin nearly knocked her socks off. Her dad would love these. Tracy bought three different types for him; much better than the traditional socks that he seemed to get from literally everybody.

The next stall along was full of handmade snow globes. Tracy hadn't had a snow globe in years. In fact, the last one she remembered was one her granddad had given her as a child. Where had it gone? She couldn't remember, but she could remember what it looked like. It was a Christmas forest scene, with Santa, his reindeer and his sleigh passing overhead. Tracy had loved it, she remembered playing with it for hours as a child. Tracy looked around the stall, hopeful there was something similar. All she saw were snowmen and Christmas trees, but no Santas. She was about to walk away from the stall when she said to the stallholder, 'You don't have any Santas do you?'

The stallholder smiled in satisfaction, 'Yes, I do! They've been very popular today; I haven't opened the new stock behind the counter. Let me do that now.' The stallholder went behind her little make-shift table and brought out a brown, cardboard box. Opening it, she brought out various different scenes containing Santa. Tracy looked through and was delighted to find one that was almost an exact replica of the one her granddad had given her all those years ago. It wasn't the original, but this one was nearly as good. Tracy bought herself the gift and the stallholder carefully wrapped it up. Stowing it securely away in her jute shopping bag, Tracy thanked her and walked towards the carol singers in the centre of the square. She was happy.

❋ ❋ ❋

Back at her flat, that afternoon, Tracy sat at her kitchen table and started wrapping the Christmas presents. The flat had an open plan living area with her sofa and TV, kitchen table and a small kitchen area at the end. Christmas jazz music was playing quietly in the background and Tracy swayed as she sellotaped. Absentmindedly, she took out the snow globe and removed it from its box. Holding it in her hands, she looked at it and remembered her dear granddad, and how enchanted she had been with the gift as a child. She remembered placing it on her bedside table at night and watching it as she went to sleep. It seemed magical to her, and touching the snow globe now, she could almost feel the same magic.

Tracy shook the snow globe in her hand and

placed it on the table as she watched the little snow flurries whirl and eddy around Santa, his sleigh, and his reindeer, flying over a snowy forest. Tracy made a wish. She said out loud, 'Santa, please bring me a gorgeous guy, all mine, just for me, one that adores me, and thinks I'm lovely. I'm tired of feeling lonely. I feel like I'm the odd one out and I'd like someone to share my life with. Thank you, Santa.' The last of the snowflakes fell and Tracy shook it again.

Tracy sat at the kitchen table, Christmas music tinkling quietly in the background, and watched the snowflakes fall. Suddenly, there was a loud knock at the door. Tracy sat up abruptly, as if she had been half in a dream. She roused herself and quickly moved the ribbon from her lap and placed the scissors back on the table.

Tracy rushed over to the front door and looking through the viewfinder she could see a man; with sandy-blonde hair, swept to one side; a trim sandy-blonde beard; and chocolate-brown eyes. His skin was slightly tanned and he had a muscly physique. He wore the most ridiculous Christmas jumper, and he was holding a key as he looked nervously about, up and down the corridor of flats. He didn't seem like he was about to burgle her, so cautiously, Tracy opened the door.

'Can I help you?' Tracy asked slowly.

The man looked at her smiling. He looked as if he had just been hit on the head and was trying to remember why he was there and what his name was.

A few seconds passed until he awkwardly sprang into action, and holding out his hand, he introduced himself, 'I'm so sorry to disturb you, my name is Will. I'm your next-door neighbour. I've just moved in today and I'm having problems with the heating. I assumed all the flats must have the same system so I was hoping you might be able to help me?'

Tracy let out a sigh of relief, and said, 'Of course, no problems at all. Let me have a look.' Tracy reached behind her to grab the door key, then stepping out, she carefully closed the flat door behind her and followed her new neighbour to the door opposite.

The flat was the mirror image of hers, but not as cosy at all. Will was right, he had just moved in today. There were boxes everywhere, and the furniture looked cold and sterile, with no pictures on the walls and no curtains at the windows. As the flat was a mirror image to hers, Tracy was able to find the heating controls and the boiler, and she showed Will exactly how it worked and how to program the temperature to his liking. Will was so nice and grateful that she forgot to be worried, and they started chatting easily. Looking around her, Tracy could see that he was in absolute chaos (although her kitchen table wasn't much better) however, neighbourly, she kindly said, 'Look, you've just moved in, from one neighbour to another, would you like to come around later and I'll cook you something to eat, so that you don't have to worry.'

Will smiled widely. He said, 'That's so kind. What a nice thing to say. Yes please.' And to affirm his yes, he nodded vigorously and smiled at Tracy.

Will seemed to have run out of words, so Tracy continued, 'Great. Shall we say about seven-thirty? Is there anything you don't like to eat? I was thinking about making a steak and kidney pie with some potatoes and fresh vegetables, if that sounds okay?' Tracy looked up enquiringly into his chocolate-brown eyes.

Will seemed to be searching for words, not knowing what to say, eventually he managed, 'Yes, yes. Thank you so much. I'll bring something for pudding.'

'But I'm supposed to be making things easy for you tonight.' Tracy smiled.

'Yes, I know, but it's the very least I can do to say thank you. I insist.' Will almost looked stern.

Tracy smiled kindly again, 'Okay, if you insist. And I'm happy to eat anything, no allergies, so bring what you want.'

Will opened the door and watched Tracy over the corridor to her flat. Tracy closed her door. On the kitchen table, the snow globe was snowing.

* * *

At seven-thirty exactly, Will knocked at Tracy's flat door. She opened it to his familiar smile, chocolate-brown eyes, and sandy-blonde hair. He was very good-looking.

Will had changed into a fresh pair of jeans, a checked shirt, and a grey cashmere crew-neck jumper. In his hands, he held his offering of a strawberry ice cream Pavlova, with real cream and strawberries on top. It looked delicious.

Tracy was starting to worry about the quality of her steak and kidney pie. At least her kitchen table was clear of presents (now stowed beneath her tiny tinsel tree in the corner) and in their place were some lit candles in a festive holder on the table. Tracy had decorated the windows with icicle fairy lights. Her new snow globe sat pride of place on the mantelpiece.

Tracy graciously ushered Will in and closed the door behind him. She placed his delicious-looking dessert in the top of her small fridge-freezer. The steak and kidney pie was resting on the side. Tracy buttered the potatoes and removed the vegetables from the hob.

As Tracy started to serve up, she noticed Will looking at the different objects on her mantlepiece. She noticed he gently picked up the Santa snow globe and shaking it, he placed it back on the mantelpiece to watch the snow fall.

Will said, 'I used to have one of these when I was a kid.' as he watched the last of the snow fall.

Tracy replied, 'My granddad gave me a very similar one when I was little. And I lost it. But I found that one at the market this morning.' Then shaking her head slightly, and almost to herself, she said, 'He always told me it was lucky, and I should make wishes on it.'

Will replied, 'And did you? Did you make a wish?'

Tracy just smiled and shook her head. She carried the plates over to the table. 'I hope you're hungry? I've given you a large slice of pie, and there's spare to take home with you if you want it?'

Will laughed and said, 'You know they say that the way to a man's heart is through his stomach.' Again, Tracy said nothing and just smiled gently and shook her head.

Will gratefully accepted a glass of red wine Tracy poured for him. Lifting his glass he said, 'Here's to new friends and good neighbours at Christmas.' Tracy repeated his sentiment as they clinked their glasses together. Outside Tracy's flat window little flakes of snow started to fall.

* * *

Tracy didn't see Will for a few days. Unfortunately, the next time she heard him, his voice was accompanied by what sounded like a woman's voice, laughing, in the corridor.

Tracy knew she was the only young woman on this level. She had assumed Will was single, just like her.

The corridor was usually very quiet. Also on this floor was Old Mr and Mrs Pennbury in the flat at the end, and just by the stairs Old Mr Michaels, who was nearly a recluse and almost never came out.

Tracy couldn't help herself; she went over to the door and had a peek through the viewfinder. She could see Will standing at his front door, the key in the lock, and next to him a beautiful lady with long, mousy-brown hair. She was wrapped up in scarves and faux furs against the heavy snow and stomping her feet, desperate to be let in to his flat. Will also wore a coat and scarf, and snow stuck in his hair. His hands were red with the cold as he fiddled with the key in the lock.

Tracy looked away. She heard the lady say, 'I'm just so excited to see your flat! I do hope you tidied up for me.'

Tracy heard Will say, 'For you, darling, anything.'

Tracy felt a physical pain in her chest. She hadn't been aware that she'd had feelings for Will. She felt like another chance at happiness had been dashed in front of her. She knew it had been too good to be true. So, he did have a girlfriend, they just weren't living together, yet. It was always the way. She thought she'd found a nice man, she thought things were going well, and then it turned out that he was taken, or gay, or wouldn't commit, and she went back to square one.

In frustration, Tracy went over to the snow globe on her mantelpiece and shook it hard saying, 'Bring me a nice, *available*, man, please?' Tracy popped the snow globe back down on the mantelpiece and watched the eddies of snow swirl around Santa.

When Tracy was depressed, she made herself a super hot-chocolate. It had whipped cream on top and was sprinkled with marshmallows; she stirred it with a special chocolate dipping wand. Cosying up on the sofa with her super hot-chocolate, Tracy flicked on the TV to find a comforting Christmas romcom and tried to feel a tiny bit better.

❋ ❋ ❋

Later that evening, Tracy heard a knock on her front door. Going over to the viewfinder she saw it was Will. She was a little surprised as she wasn't expecting to hear from him again. Shaking her head but deciding that she would always be polite, Tracy carefully opened the door and gave Will a kind smile saying, 'Is everything okay? More problems with the heating?'

Will shook his head and said, 'No the heating is working well, thank you. I'm nice and warm. I was just wondering; I have my sister to stay with me for a couple of nights, and she has forgotten her hairdryer. I don't suppose she could possibly borrow yours for half an hour? I know it's a lot to ask and we've only just met as neighbours. . .' Will's voice trailed off.

Tracy breathed a huge sigh of relief. Oh, so she was his sister. Tracy should have known. Although it wasn't to say that there weren't other women hanging around Will. She couldn't just assume. A hairdryer was no inconvenience though, she was more than willing to do that for him.

Tracy replied, 'Of course, let me fetch it now. It's no problem at all.'

Will stepped into her flat as she rushed to her bedroom to fetch her hairdryer. Winding the cord around the stem, she said, 'Here you go, no rush, I washed my hair this morning.'

Will gratefully accepted the hairdryer, and smiling, he let himself out, promising that he would be back later.

* * *

Tracy stood in front of the snow globe, in the dim evening light and said to it, 'Okay, he was available. But he hasn't exactly shown me that he's interested yet has he? It's not as if he's asked me on a date, has he?'

Tracy shook the snow globe and watched the flurries of snow twist and twizzle around Santa and his sleigh. Behind her, there was a knock at the door. Tracy went over to the viewfinder and looking through she could see Will holding the hairdryer, just as he had promised. It was rare that she came across people who kept their word. She was impressed.

Tracy opened the door to Will, who handed her the hairdryer and said, 'My sister says thank you so much and that you are literally a lifesaver.'

'Oh, not at all. Besides, it is Christmas, generosity of spirit and all that.' Tracy replied. smiling.

'Even so,' Will continued, 'my sister said that I owe you at least two favours now; for cooking me a lovely meal and lending her this hairdryer. She leaves tomorrow evening, but I was wondering if the day after that, you would like to walk around the Christmas market together? Perhaps we could find your favourite snow globe stall?'

Tracy smiled and almost laughed at the absurdity of it. Here was a gorgeous guy taking her seriously, standing by his word, turning up when he said he would, and actually asking her on what appeared to be some sort of date. Perhaps she was wrong about the snow globe, perhaps it really did grant wishes after all.

Tracy said, 'That sounds lovely. I'd love to. Thank you.'

Will gave a little fist-clench in recognition of his success, in getting her to agree to spend some time with him. Saying goodnight, he gave a small half-wave, and turned to return to his flat.

❋ ❋ ❋

Tracy wore casual attire for their Christmas market wander. She had on black jeans, which clung to the curve of her figure; a cream-coloured cashmere wool jumper with a roll neck, which also clung in all the right places; a red, three-quarter-length wool coat, trimmed with fur at the collar; and a pair of dark-brown snow boots which also had a little trim of fur around the tops. Over her long brunette hair, she wore a cream-coloured cash-mere bobble hat and matching cream-coloured cashmere gloves. Her red leather shoulder bag matched her coat. She felt festive. She still wasn't sure if this was a date or not, but she was getting to spend time with a guy that she liked and she felt excited about it. Tracy just wasn't sure if Will liked her too.

Tracy stood in front of the mantlepiece and the little snow globe. Did it really grant wishes? Shaking it gently, she said, 'If you really do grant wishes, then let tonight be the night. If Will is the one, let us kiss under a Christmas tree and then I will know, and I will be able to trust in love again.'

There was a knock at her front door. Going over to the viewfinder, Tracy saw Will was outside, twitching a little, and looking nervously up and down the corridor, before raking his fingers through his hair and checking his breath on the palm of his hand. Smiling and shaking her head she opened the door and greeted him.

Will stuttered, 'Wow, you look as cute as a little Christmas berry button!' Tracy almost laughed out loud at his crazy description of her, but she noticed he couldn't take his eyes off her too. Tracy smiled and shook her head at him, as she carefully locked the door and put her flat keys inside her little red handbag. She followed him downstairs and out into the snowy evening.

* * *

The Christmas market was just as Christmassy as it had been when she was here a week and a half ago. The same mulled wine stalls, and the same smells of home-baked goods, burgers and bangers wafted over to them. Once again, Tracy stopped at the stall with the homemade hats. She even managed to persuade Will to buy a knitted Santa hat to keep his ears warm. Laughingly, they went over to the mulled wine stall and Will bought them both a drink.

The twinkling fairy lights of the stalls lifted the navy-coloured evening light. The snow was falling gently, catching in the light of the streetlights, and landing on Tracy and Will like little Christmas wishes. Tracy felt relaxed and happy. She almost felt like this wasn't happening to her. Like it was some kind of dream. She looked around and she could see other couples, just like them, relaxed and happy, and enjoying the festive season. Everybody seemed to be full of Christmas cheer. She loved this time of year; it was her favourite season.

Will looked around and suggested, 'Why don't we go and look for your snow globe stall?'

Tracy replaced her empty, plastic, mulled wine cup back on the counter. She squeezed Will's arm and said, 'Oh yes! You'll love it. Perhaps we can get you a Santa snow globe too, and maybe your wishes could come true?'

Will laughed, 'I didn't know that they granted you wishes?'

Tracy replied, 'Well, only the ones that contain

Santas. Everybody knows that Santa grants you your wishes at Christmas.' Tracy laughed as she retraced her steps through the Christmas market to where she'd found the snow globe stall.

To Tracy's surprise, when she got to where a snow globe stall was supposed to be, she found another stall of burgers and bangers there instead, and a large queue of hungry people were waiting to be fed. She drew her eyebrows together, puzzled, and looked around thinking that she must have gone down the wrong lane. She could see the lady with the hat stand not so far away, she could see the centre of the mediaeval square where the church choir was once again singing carols. Tracy shook her head and looked back at the burger stall, concentrating hard. She was sure this was where it had been. Turning to Will she said, 'The stall was here.'

'Perhaps they've moved?' Will said helpfully.

Tracy shook her head. 'No, I was absolutely sure it was here.'

Tracy went to the neighbouring stall, which was selling Christmas tree decorations, and addressed the stallholder, 'Excuse me. Excuse me.' Tracy tried to get their attention. The customers at this stall were only browsing. Most people were queuing up next door for food.

The stallholder rushed over, hoping for a purchase. Tracy continued, 'I was wondering if you could help me? I was here just over a week ago, and there was a stall next to yours selling snow globes.

Do you know if it has moved to a different part of the market?'

The stallholder shook their head, 'Oh no, I don't think that can be right, dear. We have to book our stalls in at the start of the season, and we're here for the whole month. Once we have a pitch assigned that's it. No one else is allowed to come in.'

Tracy insisted, 'But I'm sure there was a craft stall next to you selling snow globes?'

'You must be mistaken, my dear, there are no stalls at the Christmas market selling snow globes at all. Not this year.'

Tracy was starting to feel like a lunatic, so she graciously thanked the stallholder and stopped asking questions. She turned away with a puzzled look on her face.

Will said, 'Hey little worrier.' He reached up and tried to rub the worry lines from Tracy's brow. 'It doesn't matter. We could find some snow globes another day. Let's go and listen to the choir, shall we?' He was looking down at her and smiling, but she could tell that he was slightly uneasy, as if his date was about to be spoilt over a snow globe.

Tracy smiled back, 'What a great idea.' she said, 'I must have got it wrong; it must have been a different Christmas market.' She noticed that Will looked relieved. They wandered over to the church choir singing Christmas carols in the centre of the mediaeval square. There were little charity buckets dotted around the choir, raising money for the church roof. Will pulled a couple of notes from his wallet and placed them in a bucket, making a comment that he wished he could sing as well as them.

Tracy and Will stood and listened to the carols for a little while, as the snow fell softly around them. Everything was perfectly easy and they didn't feel awkward at all, in fact quite the opposite, they were so comfortable in each other's company that if they talked, they talked, and if they didn't, they didn't, and there was no need to fill the gaps in-between. They were perfectly content to be around each other.

Will nervously pulled at his Santa hat, and looking down at Tracy he said, 'There's a beautiful Christmas tree at the edge of the square. Should we go and have a look at it? Even if your snow globes won't give me wishes, perhaps wishing on a Christmas tree might?'

Tracy smiled up at him, 'I don't want to deprive you of your Christmas wishes. Let's go over and wish on the Christmas tree.' Will greeted her answer with a wide smile.

Slowly, Tracy and Will walked through the market stalls until they reached the edge of the square. The Christmas tree was fifteen feet high, and decorated with a rainbow ribbon, giant baubles, and multicoloured Christmas lights. It had also received a dusting of snow this evening; it looked the epitome of Christmas.

Tracy said, 'Isn't it lovely? I just love Christmas, it's my favourite time of year.'

Bravely, Will said, 'Actually it's you that I think is

lovely. I couldn't believe my luck when I moved in opposite you, and finding out that you are single seems too good to be true. It's almost like fate put us together. I was just hoping that you might feel the same?' He twisted his hands and looked hopefully down at her.

Tracy couldn't believe it. It was as if everything she had wished for was being granted, like some strange, enchanted, magical land. All her wishes were coming true. Was this real? Was this really happening to her? Bravely, she grabbed her chance. Looking up at this gorgeous guy before her, the person she possibly felt most comfortable with in the world, she said, 'I think I might be falling for you too.'

In the twinkling rainbow lights of a snow-dusted Christmas tree, Will slowly leant down and kissed her.

4. CHRISTMAS ANGEL

The angel sighed wistfully, and shifted slightly on the wooden tree stump, as he pushed his feet deeper into the snow. How he wished he could join in.

In front of him was an idyllic winter scene; on a large, steep field, at the edge of the village, surrounded by trees and marked at the field base by a small, cold, stream; were children playing happily, sledging and tobogganing down the hill in the snow.

Poorer children, who couldn't afford sledges, used farmer's sacks to ride on, and had smoothed out super-fast runs, down the steep field side. It was a matter of judgement and practise to topple off the run before flying into the cold stream at the bottom of the hill (also it was highly dangerous and something that the parents would not approve of). In the confines of the village, and due to the sheer magnitude of children, the parents felt perfectly at ease to let them play, get wet and come home when they were tired.

A small boy went flying down the hill on a thick, orange-plastic, farmer's sack. He expertly tipped over at the bottom of the run to avoid the cold stream. The angel watched and sighed again wistfully, his face resting in his hands, watching over the picture-perfect Christmas scene.

Beside him, another angel arrived and said, 'My friend, Daviel, come, you are not doing the job that you have been assigned. Have you been watching the crops in the fields? Have you been watching over the farmers?'

The angel Daviel didn't bother to look away from the enchanting scene before him. Instead, he said in a quiet voice, 'I know, I know Kafziel. But it's winter. The farmers have done the heavy work during the harvest. Spring is a little way off. It's quiet now, except for a few winter potatoes.'

Kafziel looked from the magical scene in front of them to Daviel sat on a tree stump, wistfully watching the children. He said, 'We all have a job to do. Watching the children is not the job that you were assigned.'

'I know, I know. I just wish it was.'

Kafziel shook his head and disappeared.

✳ ✳ ✳

Trying to do a better job, Daviel walked around the cold barn in the night to shoo away the mice from chewing the cables in the tractor engines. It was a bit of a dull job, but he guessed someone had to do it. From behind him Kafziel arrived, and said 'Daviel, you have been summoned, you must come with me now.'

Daviel quickly shooed the last mouse away and turned around. He asked, 'What is it? Why have I been summoned?' he looked worried.

Kafziel replied, 'I cannot tell you my friend, but you must come with me now.' And he motioned to Daviel to come urgently.

* * *

Archangel Michael's eyebrows pulled together, as he looked at the angel, Daviel, before him and inquired, 'It seems that you have also been lapse in your duties protecting the farmer's fields, the crops and their equipment?'

Daviel tried to defend himself. 'It's just that, well, you see, farming isn't really my thing.'

Michael rubbed his lips and looked thoughtful. 'I see. What is it that you enjoy?' he asked.

Daviel tried to be brave as he answered truthfully, 'I love watching the children play. It's like watching little puppies playing together. They are joyous as they tumble and play, and they are so adventurous and free. . .' Daviel's voice trailed off.

Michael's eyebrows came together as he said, 'I see. You know my friend; we cannot envy humans. They're different to us, we have different jobs.'

Daviel sighed and looked at his feet as he said, 'I know, I know.' The truth was, he did envy humans. He envied their free choice and their playground on earth; he envied the way that they got to discover things and learn (even though the lessons were sometimes hard). They got to discover the beauty and magic all by themselves. Daviel watched them make choices, he watched them independently decide to be better people, to follow their hearts and their conscience, to do the best that they could. Yes, Daviel was very envious of humans.

Michael made his judgement, 'Very well. It seems that farming does not suit you, and you are very fond of children. Let's put your talents to good use. You love watching humans? Then that's what you will do. I am going to officially make you a guardian angel. A little girl is going to be born on Boxing Day in the same village that you have been watching. It is your job to be her guardian angel. You mustn't interfere, but you must always come to her aid when she asks for help. Do you understand?'

Daviel looked up, delighted, his face beamed sunshine and his aura shone in golden rays. 'Oh, thank you, thank you, Michael. I will not forget this. I will not forget that you have had faith in me.'

Michael smiled happily, 'It is not me you have to thank, it appears that this is what the creator has made you for.'

* * *

That very Christmas, on Boxing Day, a beautiful little girl, Cherry, was born into a loving family. She arrived as gently into the world as she would pass through it.

Diligently, Daviel was at her side through every faltering step, every wobbly hold of the pencil, every uncertain interaction with her friends, and every scary exam at school. Silently, eternally, he watched over the little girl with love, and proudly watched her develop and grow.

At seventeen, Cherry was a kind and loving girl. She had a curvy figure; long, dark, wavy hair; light-blue eyes; an oval, fine-featured face; and a kind, sympathetic nature, of which Daviel was proud. She had developed into a young woman. But not the young woman that her parents expected her to be.

Cherry's parents' expectations were that she would find a nice man, settle down, and have children. The difficulty was that Cherry wasn't that interested in nice men, she found herself, unexpectedly drawn to nice women, and from everything that she'd been taught from her upbringing, she knew that her feelings were not acceptable.

Cherry confessed her feelings nightly to her journal, crying as she wrote. Standing next to her, unseen, Daviel cried too.

Daviel knew it could be challenging being a guardian angel, but he never expected this. Cherry was the person that Daviel loved most in this universe, excepting their creator, and he would have done everything and anything to save her from this pain, but until she asked for help, he was helpless to help her. He was duty-bound to painfully stand by and watch.

* * *

It was the start of December. Everybody was excited for Christmas, and this year there was an added celebration: on Boxing Day, Cherry would turn eighteen. An adult launched into the world to be her own independent person. To do as she wished. To choose her own path and destiny, and love whomsoever she might choose. Cherry had just returned from her first term at university, and fate had bestowed on Cherry something so unimaginably beautiful she could hardly believe it was happening to her. She had fallen in love.

Cherry had met Sally at the fresher's fair. There was an instant connection between them. Although they were on different courses, whenever they weren't in lectures or doing assignments on the computers, they would spend the rest of their time together. They explored the city of Bath, went clubbing together, shopping together, and a few weeks after meeting, they tenderly shared their first kiss. Everything about their relationship was magical, until the end of the autumn term and it was time to return home for Christmas. Sally's parents were happy to accept Sally just as she was, and were happy to accept Cherry too. However, this was not the case for Cherry.

In her bedroom, in hushed tones, Cherry spoke to Sally over video call. 'How was your Christmas?'

Cherry asked.

Sally's cheery face reached out to Cherry over the video call, as she said, 'It's been great seeing family! We've had a lovely Christmas, but I miss you so much.'

Cherry cradled the phone to her, as she said, 'I miss you so much that it hurts. I haven't spoken to my parents about you, I'm really worried.'

Sally tried to comfort Cherry by saying, 'It's going to be fine, don't worry. Do you want me to come over?'

Cherry shook her head, 'I know I must face this alone. I must be brave and do it. I appreciate your support though.'

Sally was physically upset to see Cherry crying and said, 'Cherry. Cherry, whatever happens, I'm always going to be here for you. If your parents don't take it well, then I can come and pick you up, and you can come here. My mum and dad are desperate to meet you, and they're so happy that we've found each other. They can tell that we're in love. I want you to know that whatever happens, I'm not going to abandon you, and you have a place with me, okay?'

Tears streaked down Cherry's cheeks as she nodded silently to the phone and said, 'Yes, I understand, thank you, Sal. I am afraid, but I know that we're supposed to be together. I just need to find a way through this.'

Sally replied, 'How I wish I was there with you right now, giving you a cuddle. Look let's try to think of happier things. Happy birthday for to-morrow, eh? I hope you have an amazing day, and we'll talk on the phone tomorrow hey? We'll catch up?'

Again, Cherry nodded silently to the phone, before gathering the courage to say the words, 'Yes, I'll text you, and let's talk tomorrow, that will make me feel better.' Cherry tried to smile and waved goodbye.

Unseen, Daviel sat next to Cherry on her bed. He put his arm around her. Daviel's mouth was set in a tight line. He knew how strictly religious Cherry's parents were. He had a bad feeling about this.

❊ ❊ ❊

The next morning, Cherry descended the stairs for breakfast, followed by Daviel. His heart and steps were heavy. Daviel knew what Cherry was just about to do.

At the breakfast table, Daviel watched his beautiful Cherry sit down. Cherry's father was scrolling on his phone, he looked up to wish her happy birthday. Taking a big gulp of tea, Cherry cleared her throat and said, 'I have something important to tell you both.' Her mum was buttering her toast and her dad put his cup down, they both turned to look at her expectantly, looking for news of a boyfriend.

Cherry took a deep, shaky breath and said, 'I'm gay.'

The silence in the room was as if all the air had turned to lead and fallen on the sound waves. Cherry didn't move, as she watched in slow motion the horrified reactions of her parents. Her mum dropped the butter knife and her father looked like he was about to explode. Her mum started crying hysterically, and she brought her hand to her eyes as she said repeatedly, 'No, no. Oh, no, no, no, Cherry, not my Cherry.'

Cherry's dad instantly got up from his place at the table, and she wondered for a moment if he was about to come over and hit her, but instead, he went straight to his wife and wrapped his arms around her.

Cherry was like a rat out of a trap. She dashed from the breakfast table to her bedroom and shut the door closed. She was shaking with terror; she had hoped her parent's response would be something similar to Sally's parents. This was not the life she wanted. She should have guessed it would be like this. Cherry should have realised that her parents wouldn't understand how she felt. She was a failure. Cherry had cut herself off from her parents forever, and now she could never live the life she had hoped. Her dreams were shattered.

Cherry wedged her chest of drawers against her bedroom door, barricading herself in. Going towards the wardrobe, she pulled out all her shoes, and grabbing her childhood blanket she climbed inside, shutting the doors behind her. Cherry could hear her phone on her bed buzzing, she knew it was Sally, checking to see how the talk had gone this morning. Cherry didn't feel like she could connect with Sally or anyone else. She wished she'd never been born. She wished this wasn't her life.

Outside the wardrobe, looking sadly at the closed doors, his head bowed and tears streaming down his cheeks, was the person who loved Cherry most in the world, and there was nothing he could say or do to help her. Daviel searched through his powers, desperately thinking what he was allowed to do. Daviel thought and thought, but he could find nothing.

Silently, Daviel entered through the doors and sat on the opposite side of the wardrobe to Cherry, watching her sobbing herself into a little ball. His beautiful little Cherry was in pain. Daviel didn't know that his fate was to watch the person he loved most in the world kill herself, while he was helpless to stop her. He felt his heart start to fall through his body.

Slowly, Cherry pulled out the five packets of paracetamol that she'd stowed away. Daviel watched as she methodically popped out the pills. Eventually, she held a pile of white pills in her hands. Daviel was reminded of her holding a handful of snowflakes to show her mum when she was a little girl. Cherry started to put the pills into her mouth. Each time she said, 'I wish I'd never been born.'

Daviel swiped at the pills, he tried to push her hand over, but nothing happened. Desperately, he tried to think of a solution. He was not allowed to leave her side, he had to stay here. In the darkest moment of their lives, he called out to his friend Kafziel to come to him, he called to Michael to save her.

There was an audible thud outside the wardrobe. Daviel stepped outside to see Kafziel and Michael. They looked worried.

Kafziel grasped Daviel's hand and asked, 'How is she?'

Daviel replied, 'I can't stop her. Please help me.'

Michael reached out his hand and placed it on Daviel's forehead saying, 'Try this.'

Daviel nodded and rushed back into the wardrobe. He reached forward and wrapping his arms around his beautiful Cherry he said, 'Come with me.'

Cherry stood, hand in hand with a man she'd never met before. He was nondescript. He wore a brown suit and had short brown hair. He was slightly shorter than average, and had a kind face. Even though she didn't know him, Cherry felt comfortable as she held his hand. She turned to him and asked, 'Why am I here?'

The man smiled kindly at her, and tugging at her hand, they walked together along the hospital corridor. Coming to the end of the corridor they peeked through a window into the neonatal ward, where they could see a lady cradling a tiny baby. The lady was her mum. The little baby was Cherry.

Cherry said in shock to the gentleman, 'It's my mum!' He nodded and smiled. Cherry looked back to the scene of a mother enraptured with her new-born child.

Suddenly they were outside. It was summer and Cherry was walking along the edge of a lake. She turned to her companion; he was still holding her hand. She said to him, 'This is where I used to go as a little girl.'

He smiled and said, 'Yes, that's right. Do you re-member?'

Slowly they walked towards one of the small fish-ing piers at the edge of the lake. Cherry gasped as she saw a little six-year-old girl with her father, who was diligently tying her fly so that she could swish the tiny line out into the middle of the lake and try to catch a fish. Cherry's father stroked her head lovingly and stood back as she tried to cast.

Cherry looked fondly at the scene before them, as dragonflies flew past their faces, 'I used to be here for hours with Dad.' she said.

'Yes, that's right. Did you know that these are some of his most cherished memories?'

Cherry looked up at the man and shook her head saying, 'No, I didn't know that. He never said.' She looked back at the scene, just as it disappeared.

Cherry and the man were in her university halls of residence. Her parents had just said goodbye to Cherry, and she was waving goodbye to them as they walked away down the corridor. But rather than seeing the retreating backs of her parents, she saw her mum's face wet with tears, and trying not to spoil Cherry's moment of freedom. Her mum was crying because she was saying goodbye to her beautiful little girl who no longer needed her. Stoically, her father held her mum's hand and comforted her, before turning back to give Cherry a wave goodbye. Further down the corridor, another fresher was just moving into her room. She turned to look at Cherry standing in the doorway of her room. Her eyes were transfixed by Cherry, it was love at first sight. The young woman was Sally.

Cherry and the man were walking towards the university. The man still held Cherry's hand as they followed Sally as she walked to one of her lectures. Beside Sally, one of the boys from her course said, 'Hey let's go on a date.' Sally ignored him. He continued, 'I've seen you looking at that girl. What's wrong with me!' He started shouting at Sally as she tried to walk faster to get away from him. 'Hey, what's wrong with a man!'

Bravely, Sally turned to him and said, 'You wouldn't know what true love was if it got up and bit you.' Then she swore at him and stared him down until he left her alone and went away. Laughing at Sally as he did so.

Cherry and the man were back in Cherry's bedroom at her parent's house. They were outside her wardrobe. The man opened the wardrobe door and she could see her limp body on the wardrobe floor, surrounded by little white pills. Someone at the bedroom door was banging it. Someone was trying to get in.

Outside her room, Cherry heard the desperate voice of Sally at the door shouting, 'Cherry! Cherry!'

Cherry's dad was trying to push the door in. He threw the full force of his body against the door, but Cherry had barricaded it too well. They couldn't get in. Sally was hysterical. Her mum was hugging her arms, crying.

Cherry turned in horror to her companion and asked, 'What have I done?'

Sadly, he raised his eyes to hers and shook his head.

Desperately, Cherry said, 'I take it back, I want to live!' Imploringly, she looked into his eyes, 'Please will you help me?'

❋ ❋ ❋

Cherry awoke in a hospital bed. Tubes and monitors surrounded her. It was dark outside. Collapsed on the side of her bed, sleeping with exhaustion, with her arms spread over Cherry's legs and clutching a wet, mascara-stained tissue, was Sally. At the far end of her bed, sat in chairs along the opposite wall, sat her mum and dad. They were sleeping lightly, their hands held in support over the adjoining arms of their chairs.

Inside her body, Cherry felt sore, and she had a horrendous migraine. Cherry raised her eyes, and taking in her surroundings she looked over at the door. A man stood quietly in the doorway. He was wearing a nondescript brown suit and had a gentle face. He watched her with kind eyes. Cherry made a huge effort to try and talk, but she couldn't. Her throat felt as if it was made of knives.

Desperately, Cherry mouthed the words, "Thank you."

The man seemed to disappear.

Leaning back onto her pillows, Cherry fell back into an exhausted sleep, protected by the people that loved her most in the world.

5. SANTA, PLEASE BRING MUMMY A NEW DADDY THIS CHRISTMAS

Dear Santa,

I have been a good girl this year, so I want to ask for something really, really big. It's not for me, it's for my mummy. Mummy works very hard, all the time, and she buys my sister and I nice things. When I go to bed, I can hear her doing the washing up and ironing our clothes. Mummy never grumbles, but she looks tired and sometimes falls asleep in front of the TV. Santa, I thought it would be nice if you could give her a daddy this Christmas so that he could take her out to the pub, like all the other mummies and daddies, and then she could wear a sparkly dress and look pretty. Also, he could help her with the washing up.

Thank you, Santa,

Lots of love, Eloise Richards

* * *

Neil didn't mind mopping up some of the issues from Christmas Eve. To be honest, he was glad of the money, and it wasn't as if he had anyone close to share Christmas with. His mum had died five years ago and his dad had passed away when he was a teenager. He had a sister, but she was up in Sheffield, and Devon was a long way from Sheffield, even though he was used to driving as part of his job.

Neil rubbed his neat beard in an absentminded way, as he spoke to his boss on the phone. 'Yes, it's just the five packages but they are dotted around like points on a star. One of them looks like it's been passed around a football pitch. . .' Neil prodded the package with the point of his foot. He'd have to tape that one before he put it in the van.

While Neil continued to talk to his boss, he caught a glimpse of his reflection in the van window. He had sparkling hazel eyes; and a kind, warm, tanned, squarish face; which was complimented by his light-brown eyebrows; and light-brown wavy hair. He wore his beard trimmed neatly around his face. He was just short of six feet tall and his preference was to wear a pair of jeans and a comfy hoodie, but as he was a delivery van driver rushing around, most of the day, he tended to wear shorts on the job, unless it got really cold, and this winter was really cold.

Leaning outside the door of the open warehouse at the end of the industrial estate, Neil could see a few snowflakes falling. It was seven-thirty in the morning, Christmas morning.

Yesterday had been absolute chaos at the delivery depot and there were always a few mistakes. Neil didn't mind clearing up the last of the problems, he got paid quadruple-time and, more than that, he felt the satisfaction of completing the job, and making people happy. Neil liked making people happy.

Neil continued to talk to his boss, 'Yeah, yeah, no problems. . . I don't mind mate. . . cheers. . . yeah, I'll pick up a turkey sandwich from the garage on you then. . . Ha ha ha. . . all right. . . yeah, yeah, I'll take tomorrow off. . . yeah, okay, all right, see you in a couple of days mate. . .' Neil pressed the red button on his mobile, and using his handheld device, checked in the five packages still to be delivered, before loading them into his van. Closing the doors to the depot, Neil headed out in this white van, to deliver, just like Santa, the five missing presents.

❋ ❋ ❋

The first present was Neil's favourite sort of job; an old lady, alone at Christmas, and he was delivering her daughter's present from Australia. Apparently, it contained cards and homemade gifts from the grandchildren. Neil couldn't be happier, he knew he'd made her Christmas, and he was quite happy to accept the warm mince pies that she loaded him up with for the rest of his journey. Not long after that, he pulled over and had a mug of coffee from his thermos and ate one of her homemade mince pies.

In the distance, Neil could hear the church bells starting to ring in Christmas Day and calling people to come and sing carols. He wasn't churchy, but he did believe in goodness. He loved his job and he couldn't imagine doing anything else.

The second present was a mountain bike. This was the battered package, and the teenage boy, who was the recipient, was upset the bike might have been damaged.

Neil and the boy's dad carefully checked the package and opened it up to inspect the bike: cutting off the brown cardboard and finding, miraculously, underneath, an unblemished and very expensive mountain bike. It was a present from his dad so that the two of them could go mountain biking together. The boy was overjoyed and obviously very excited about his present.

The boy's dad suggested that they have a quick bike out together before his mum finished cooking lunch, and the boy happily agreed.

The dad shook Neil by the hand and thanked him for coming out on Christmas morning to make sure his son got the delayed present. Neil brushed away the thanks and tried not to blush as he happily walked back to his van.

The third present was a coveted new edition Xbox, being delivered to a very excited nine-year-old, who thought that he wasn't going to get his Christmas present this year.

His parents were overwhelmed by Neil's kindness. It was just after lunch on Christmas Day, and the boy's dad tried to slip Neil a little bit of money to say thank you. But Neil shook his head graciously and declined.

Neil said, 'Thank you, but it's all right, it's part of the service. I don't mind delivering today, it makes me happy. Give it to charity if you like.'

The two men nodded at each other in understanding. They were both good men, the types who kept the cogs of society turning and the wheels of decency spinning, the types of men who made sure that everyone was happy and everything was right.

The last two presents looked the same. They appeared to be work hampers that hadn't been delivered but contained perishable goods with a tight delivery deadline. They needed to be out today. Neil didn't mind that his company didn't do work hampers, he was glad of the cash bonus instead, then he could spend it on what he wanted.

Neil tapped his tracker and let his sat-nav direct him to the next drop-off.

The penultimate delivery of the hamper was to a single lady in a flat. She looked as though she was a little merry from drinking champagne and watching Christmas romcoms. Neil carried the heavy hamper into her flat for her, and politely declined when she tried to encourage him to join her for a Christmas drink. He would never drink and drive, he had a responsibility to society.

Cheekily, she stole a kiss on Neil's cheek under the mistletoe at her front door. Considering she was single, he correctly guessed it was a booby trap for any single male that happened to pass by.

In a smooth move, Neil managed to duck out underneath her clinching arms, and protest, saying he had to get his last delivery done. Gratefully, he scuttled down the path steps and back to the safety of his van. A small bead of sweat ran along his brow as she came out to wave goodbye.

Just one package left to deliver. The light was starting to fade as the sun began to dip towards the horizon in a pool of peaches-and-pinks. The last package was a little bit of a drive, to the seaside town of Newton Sunbury, but it would be worth it to complete the job.

Neil loved driving along the roads and seeing the Christmas trees proudly standing in the house windows. Especially at twilight, when people hadn't closed their curtains yet, and it all looked cosy and Christmassy. Neil liked it when people were happy. It made him feel good.

Neil glanced at the address on the screen for the last package. Newton Sunbury was a lovely little Victorian town, overlooking the coast. Not too far from home. Neil started imagining getting back to his warm little cottage later tonight. He'd probably have a nice dram of whiskey, just like his dad used to at Christmas, then he'd heat up his microwaveable Christmas meal and watch a silly film. But not until he delivered his last package and seen the smile on the customer's face.

The snow was continuing to fall lightly. The snow hadn't caused much trouble on the roads today because it hadn't been thick enough to stay, the roads had just been a bit slushy. Neil was always a careful driver and would shake his head at the "one-speed-all-condition drivers".

Neil drove into the small town of Newton Sunbury. Small flurries of snowflakes danced in the light of the streetlights, and lines of lit Christmas trees were shining out from house windows to welcome him into the town. He almost felt like he was coming home.

Nineteen Westweek Close. That was the one. Neil could see the lights were on in the Victorian terraced house. Always a good sign. He pulled back the van door and deftly lifting the very heavy package, closed the van door. He securely held his tracker as he navigated his way towards the front gate, and up the garden path to the front door.

On the door was a multicoloured bauble wreath. The door was painted bright red, it looked cosy and welcoming. Ringing the doorbell and knocking as well (just in case the occupants had had a couple of drinks), Neil manhandled the package in his arms, and waited patiently for someone to answer. His muscly arms held the package firmly, and he could hear somebody pulling back the security chain on the other side of the door.

The door sprang open.

In front of Neil, haloed by the light of the hall, was a slim woman, wearing a cosy, cream-coloured, Christmas jumper and knitted jogging bottoms. She had bare feet with pink nail varnish on her toes and pink nail varnish on the nails of her slim, elegant fingers. Her face was heart-shaped, and just like him, she had hazel eyes. Her lips were slim and her cheekbones high. Her hair was dyed dark-red and her eyebrows were dark brown. She looked at him in surprise, so Neil tried to explain that he had a perishable package for her. As he did so, she gave him the most incredible smile, revealing her small, white teeth.

Neil struggled for breath and struggled to find his words in equal measure. Stumbling over his words he said, 'I, I, this was at the depot and it's perishable, I think it's a company hamper or something like that? I just wanted to get it out to you by Christmas Day.'

Behind the lady, in the hall, two little girls appeared. They stood agog, staring at him. Neil focussed his attention back on the lady and bravely asked, 'Perhaps I could get your husband to carry it in? Or do you want me to put this in the hall for you?'

The lady pulled back from the door as she said, 'No husband, no partner. I'm single. Please dump it in the hall, just there. I really appreciate it.' As

Neil placed the package where requested she continued, 'Thank you so much. You must be freezing? Delivering packages on Christmas Day too. You must have such a good heart.'

Neil didn't know what to say. He muttered something and looked at his shoes, while jabbing the handheld controller at her, and saying, 'Please, could you sign here?' His breath and words were catching in his throat, and he thought he was about to choke.

The lady sprang into action, her pink-nailed, manicured hand dashing over the screen like sparklers whizzing around in the darkness on bonfire night.

Neil was mesmerised. He didn't know what to do. He felt as though he'd been hit over the head by a big club. He wished he could make time stop, but what could he do? He had to go. This wasn't his place. He was just a delivery driver. Besides, the company had very strict policies on things like this.

Pulling his courage to him as best he could, Neil managed to look down into her eyes and said, 'Thank you. That's great. Happy Christmas.'

The beautiful lady, smiled up at him as she said, 'Merry Christmas to you too, and thank you so much for coming. You really are so kind. I'm glad that people like you exist in the world.'

From behind her, one of the little girls looked confused and stepped towards him from behind her mother, to stare at Neil. Neil blushed and said,

'Well, I guess I better go. Good night and Happy Christmas again.'

How Neil's legs walked him away, he didn't know. He walked carefully back down the path, and into his van, where he sat, gasping for breath, his body numb with shock. Never in his life had something like that happened to him, and the question was: What on earth was he going to do about it? Neil's company had strict policies about things like this. He couldn't stalk her. He couldn't look her up in the directory.

Glancing over to the tracker on the stand in his van, Neil knew that this was the last moment he would ever see her details, and guiltily, before he pressed "delivery done", he reread her name and memorised her address: Natasha Richards, Nineteen Westweek Close, Newton Sunbury, Devon.

* * *

Neil couldn't wait to get into work on the 27 December. His boss insisted that he take Boxing Day off, but it had been agony. Neil knew he just needed to find a way to get back to her. To Newton Sunbury. Legitimately. If he could do deliveries in the area, he might be lucky and he might come across Natasha again.

Neil checked the delivery area he had been given for today and found that he was going to be working fifty miles east. He was gutted. Life couldn't just present him with this woman and then torture him by taking her away? He had to find a way to see her again. Noticing that Mark was doing deliveries around the area of Newton Sunbury, he went over to him.

Neil asked, 'Hey mate, I see you're in the Newton Sunbury area today? I don't suppose you'd fancy swapping delivery routes? I was hoping to be over that way.'

Mark shook his head sadly, 'Sorry Neil, normally I'd say yes, but I've asked for the area specifically because the missus and the kids are visiting a cousin. I'm going to meet them after the deliveries are done to pick them up in the van and drive us home. I can't do it. I'm sorry.'

Neil felt sick to the pit of his stomach. It was agony not seeing her for yet another day. He put on his best smile and said, 'Oh, no worries, it's okay. I'll see about another day.'

Neil didn't have any luck the rest of the week either. As the delivery routes came in each morning and the packages piled up, Neil seemed to get unluckier and unluckier. He couldn't get over to Newton Sunbury at all.

Neil started to worry. What if somebody else should find her? And see how wonderful she was? And ask her on a date, or ask her to be their girlfriend? What was he going to do? He might lose her forever.

Neil's brain set to work on how he was going to crack this puzzle. It seemed like he wasn't going to get the opportunity to deliver her something again, and all his attempts to get over to Newton Sunbury with a delivery route were not working out at all. He had to think of another way.

* * *

Neil had the day off. He couldn't help it; he took himself to the nearest florist and bought a big bunch of roses. It was the 30 December and he knew, he just knew, that this lady was the one for him. Somehow, he just had to hope that she would see it too. He didn't yet know what he was going to say and he was scared, but he was more scared of losing her.

Neil got into his BMW car and carefully drove out to Newton Sunbury; the roads were still slushy. His plan was to hang around the town and see if she happened to walk through town with her daughters. If not, he might just walk along her street. Just once. Neil didn't like stalkers, those men were creeps, but he needed to create an opportunity where he got to ask her, just once, if she would consider him. Then he would know. Hopefully, she wouldn't be angry.

The Christmas sales were in full swing in the little town of Newton Sunbury. The town was full of bijoux boutiques, specialist food and cake shops and children's toy shops, all trying to shed their Christmas wares at knockdown prices.

Neil wandered around for a couple of hours in the cold, but he didn't see Natasha or her little daughters. He was starting to feel cold and deflated. He didn't know what to do, he didn't want to walk up her street. He didn't want to be accused of being a stalker or lose his job. That would be the worst outcome. Neil thought sadly that he was just a delivery driver. What did he have to offer her? She probably would say, "No." anyway. Who would want him?

Sitting in his cold car, Neil's fears got the better of him. He decided that the best thing to do would be to turn around and go home.

* * *

Neil sat dejectedly in front of the TV, with his microwave dinner on his lap, and the bunch of roses sitting in the bath, undelivered. It didn't seem right for the delivery not to make its destination. He was used to completing the job, he was used to giving gifts and making people happy. Neil didn't feel right at all, in fact, he was starting to feel a little down, and that wasn't like him. He was always so happy.

Grabbing his mobile, Neil rang his sister; his last proper family. She'd know what to say.

Hearing the phone ring on the other end of the line, Neil waited patiently for his sister to pick up, and when she did and cheerfully called down the phone to him, Neil answered, 'Sis, I don't know what to do. Please help me.' His voice was full of pain and anguish. He felt like this was the worst moment of his life; like he'd lost everything and he didn't know what to do anymore.

* * *

Neil felt a hundred times better after talking to his sister and getting a woman's opinion on how to be asked out for a date. Neil decided, with the advice of his sister, to try the same plan again. He was going to drive back to Newton Sunbury, he'd check around the shops first, then, if he didn't see Natasha and her daughters, he'd go to her front door to ask her out for a coffee, just once, and hope that she wouldn't report him.

Carefully removing the roses from the boot of his car. Neil parked up in the Council car park and navigated his way over the slushy pavements into town. He slowly walked along the high street, then he turned to go back the other way.

Neil's breath caught in his throat; there she was! Coming down the pavement with her two daughters, carrying some shopping bags. Her dark-red hair peeked out from under a cream bobble hat, she had a cream scarf wrapped around her neck, and a small grey coat over her cream, knitted, jogging bottoms and a pair of biker boots.

Of course, she was going to say, "No." but he had to know. Neil needed to complete the job; make his delivery and find out. This was his chance, as his mum had always told him, "Aim for the Moon, and even if you miss, you will land amongst the stars."

Neil crossed the road and walked along the wide, rural-town pavement, towards Natasha and her daughters. When he approached the small group, Natasha looked up with a beautiful smile on her face as she said, 'Oh! You're the lovely delivery man who was out on Christmas Day, aren't you? I didn't realise you lived around here?' Behind her, one of the little girls looked at him then nudged and looked quizzically at her sister. They were the image of their mother.

Natasha continued to smile at Neil kindly.

Neil nearly choked, but he was determined, and he'd memorised the words his sister had told him to say. He'd carefully practised them again and again. Neil's brain barely engaged, as he said from his script, 'I hope you don't mind, and I don't want you to think anything of it, but I think you are the most beautiful lady I've ever met, and I was hoping that you would accept this gift of some roses. Just because it's Christmas.'

Natasha gasped in surprise, mirrored by the surprise of her eldest daughter, and contrasted against the massive smile on the face of her youngest daughter. Neil looked back at Natasha's beautiful hazel eyes, and tried to appear normal, smiley and kind.

Natasha reached up to accept the flowers from him. 'They're beautiful.' She said, smelling them. 'I've never received such a lovely gift. Thank you so much. What a nice thing to say.'

Neil looked at his feet and squashed some slush

away on the pavement with the toe of his trainers. 'Well,' he stuttered, 'It's nothing really, I just that I thought you are very beautiful, and I didn't know how else to tell you.'

Natasha held the bunch of red roses in her arms. She smiled widely and a small tear appeared at the corner of her eye. She said, 'I don't think anyone has ever given me such a beautiful gift.'

Looking back at Neil thoughtfully, as he stood there, embarrassed and looking at his feet, Natasha said, 'Would you like to join my daughters and I for a coffee and a cake? We were just heading to our favourite café.'

Neil couldn't believe it. He'd hardly dared hope that this would be her answer. He was so happy that he could barely get the words, "Yes" and "Thank you" out.

Natasha pointed up the street. On the left was a little café, with a few wooden benches outside, and imitation cakes hanging from the sign. Its square of the pavement was demarked by faux box trees in planters, festively covered in Christmas lights. She said, 'That café's our favourite. Do you mind if we go there?'

Neil smiled and said, 'Not at all.' And before he could stop himself, he added, 'I just can't believe that a lovely lady like you is single.'

A small cloud passed over Natasha's face. She explained, 'After my car accident, my husband said that he didn't want to be stuck with an invalid for the rest of his life. To be honest, I lost my faith in men after that.' Her eldest daughter reached out a hand and placed it on her mum's shoulder. Her youngest daughter looked sad.

Neil took a sharp intake of breath and said without thinking, 'The guy is an idiot, he doesn't have eyes.' Before he could say anything else to incriminate himself, Neil clamped his mouth closed.

Natasha's beautiful laugh rang out over the pavement, as she said, 'You must be one of the nicest men I've ever met.'

'Not me.' Neil shook his head, as he went around to the back of her wheelchair to take over from her daughters and push Natasha along the pavement. 'I just like being helpful and useful. I say things as I see them. I'm probably a bit too open. I hope you don't mind me telling you that I think you are lovely, do you?'

Natasha and her daughters laughed at the beautiful compliment, and with the release of nerves. Natasha said, 'You really are a diamond. How did you find me? I don't even know your name!'

Neil said, 'I'm Neil Strong.' He reached over her shoulder to shake her hand. 'I guess I must just have followed my Christmas present package tracker to find you.'

They all laughed. As they reached the café, Natasha said, 'Eloise, would you hold the door?' Her youngest daughter helpfully pulled the door back, as Neil carefully pushed her wheelchair over the step, into the cosy atmosphere of the café.

6. THE OTHER WOMAN

Kirsty knew that this was the year Peter would propose. So, by the time it got around Christmas and Peter still hadn't got down on one knee, it seemed for certain that he would ask her either at Christmas or New Year.

In the week running up to Christmas, Peter wasn't his normal self. Every now and again he would turn to Kirsty, and push back some of her blonde hair from her wavy bob, back over her ear; or look into her sparkling blue eyes, matched by his own light-blue eyes, and say, 'This is our first Christmas together in our own home.' or add, 'I'm so happy, just the two of us. Aren't you?' or, 'We're so happy together.'

In reply, Kirsty would ruffle his short brown hair and say, 'You silly. You know I love you to bits.' Then she would kiss her finger and tap it to the end of his nose.

It was the day before Christmas Eve. Kirsty and Peter were cuddled up together on the sofa in their tiny cottage. In front of them, the TV was playing a cheesy Christmas film, and beside them the wood burner roared away, dancing out its orange heat. Their feet were resting on the coffee table, upon which was an open box of posh chocolates and a half-drunk bottle of wine. In the corner, a small Christmas tree sparkled with chasing rainbow lights and a selection of sparkly decorations.

Deliberately reaching forward for the TV controls, Peter turned off the TV, and turned to Kirsty. Clearing his throat he said, 'Kirsty, there's something really important that I need to talk to you about.'

Kirsty's breath became heavier and her heart started beating out of her chest. Their life together was perfect. They'd just started renting their first house together. It was a little cottage along a small farm lane at the edge of a village, just the right size for two young lovers. They'd also discussed getting a dog soon, when they bought their own house. They were saving for a deposit and being careful with their money. Everything was coming together. They were so happy. Kirsty knew what he was about to say.

Peter cleared his throat again and said, 'I had a phone call this morning.' He paused significantly and lifting Kirsty's hand, held it gently between his, as he looked her in the eyes and said, 'I know this isn't what you expected, and I'm sorry that this has come so close to Christmas, but my mum was in tears this morning on the phone. She misses my dad and she feels terribly alone. I'm so sorry I didn't have a chance to talk with you about this, and I hope it's okay... I feel so close to you and

I feel like we support each other through every-thing, and I know that you regard family highly. . . so I told her not to worry and she could stay with us for Christmas. I hope that's all right?'

Kirsty took a big gulp of air. She liked Peter's mum the handful of times she'd met her. She was quite a strong character but also charming and ex-troverted. It wasn't exactly what she'd planned for Christmas, or what she secretly hoped Peter was going to ask her. He was right though. Family is family, and if his mum needed to stay, and she was lonely, then Kirsty certainly felt that it was their duty to offer her a warm hug and somewhere to be over Christmas.

Kirsty couldn't help but feel disappointed, but she tried to hide it as she replied, 'Oh, Lovely, of course, we need to support each other, and I know how close you are to your mum. I wouldn't want her feeling upset and lonely over Christmas and she's only one extra mouth to feed. I'm sure we can stretch what we have and make it a nice Christmas for her too.'

Peter spontaneously hugged her and kissed Kirsty's forehead, then held her back from him as he said, 'I don't know many girls like you, who would be so understanding. I do appreciate it. You're one in a million darling.' He kissed her on the forehead again.

Kirsty heart sunk a little. This wasn't the Christ-mas she had planned at all.

* * *

The very next morning, at nine a.m. sharp, Peter's mum arrived in her old Volvo estate, with three suitcases and some re-useable supermarket bags full of presents. Luckily, Peter and Kirsty had rushed to get out of bed and get washed half an hour before, so by the time she came to the front door they were relaxed and presentable.

Peter helped his mum, Heather, with her bags, and Kirsty welcomed her into their cottage; showing her the spare bedroom and offering to make her a cup of tea or coffee and something for breakfast.

Kirsty smiled at Heather warmly, and lightly touching her arm, said, 'I'll put the hot water on for a cuppa and perhaps you'd like a warm croissant or some toast and butter when you've settled in and you're ready to come downstairs?'

Heather looked around the spare bedroom and said, 'Oh, what a sweet, *little* room. Is this the one that you said was used as a study? It's amazing you can fit a single bed sideways in it, but you've managed to squeeze it in I see.' She gave the mattress a testing prod with her hand. Kirsty could hear Peter bringing in the last of her bags, downstairs. Heather continued, 'And we're sharing a bathroom, are we? It's the one that's opposite my door, is it?'

Kirsty could feel her cheeks starting to burn red.

She felt ashamed that the room was a little too small, and she wished there was a separate bathroom for Peter's mum to use. Kirsty scolded herself, thinking she'd need to remember to clean her toiletries away after her showers.

Smiling kindly, Kirsty replied, 'Yes, we just have the one bathroom in this little cottage, but I've managed to housetrain Peter! I promise he won't make a mess.' and made a half-laugh at her own joke.

Heather drew her eyebrows together in confusion, 'Housetrain him? Isn't that something you do with dogs?'

Kirsty tried to pass her comment off with a half-hearted laugh saying, 'Yes it's just a joke.'

Heather said, 'Oh yes, one of those ones that I don't understand.' She patted Kirsty on the arm and continued, 'I don't get the younger generation these days. Silly me!' and smiled at her.

Heather looked beyond Kirsty's shoulder, trying to peek across the corridor, into the bathroom opposite. Kirsty took the hint and said, 'Let me show you the bathroom.'

Kirsty moved into the corridor, and opening a small cupboard, she showed Heather where the towels were stored and explained that there was a towel on the bed in her room too. Then she moved aside to let Heather inspect the very small bathroom, with a shower, basin and toilet.

Heather said, 'Oh, I didn't realise there wasn't a bathtub.' And by way of explanation again held

Kirsty's forearm as she explained, 'I always have a bath on a Saturday morning. It's my only treat.'

'Yes,' Kirsty said, 'We haven't got a bathtub, unfortunately. It's just a little cottage.' Kirsty twisted her hands together and she tried to think of something else to say.

Heather filled the pause agreeing with her saying, 'Yes, it is just a little cottage, isn't it? Very sweet.'

Embarrassed, Kirsty added, 'Well, we are thinking of trying to buy our first place together next year.'

Heather looked surprised, and said, 'Oh! Are you? That's strange, Peter always mentions everything of importance to me, I wonder why he wouldn't mention that?' She gently shook her head.

Kirsty didn't know what to say or do. She felt twisted and in a jumble. Trying to think of something to say, she suggested, 'Would you like something to drink or eat? A croissant or some toast perhaps, or some fruit?'

Heather replied, 'Oh yes, that sounds lovely. I'll come downstairs in five minutes. A croissant will do. I forget you young girls don't bake anymore. I'm quite surprised Peter has stayed with you so long as has, because he loves his home cooking.' She smiled kindly at Kirsty. Kirsty was being dismissed.

Unsteadily, Kirsty said, 'Great! I'll get the croissant warmed. Well, I'll see you downstairs in a minute.' Kirsty descended the tiny wooden staircase into the living room.

The Christmas tree was merrily flashing rainbow colours at her. Peter was by the front door with three suitcases and five shopping bags which were full of presents and other assorted household items. Kirsty surveyed the bags and thought to herself, "It's only going to be for a few days. Perhaps Heather iss one of those ladies who never travels light?"

Peter closed the front door, blocking out the cold, and smiled encouragingly over at Kirsty saying, 'Thanks love. This means so much to me. Is Mum settling in okay upstairs?'

Kirsty smiled uncertainly at him. 'Yes, she seems to be doing well. I'm going to put on a pot of tea. Would you like a cuppa?'

Peter replied, 'Oh I'll have a coffee actually, the same as Mum prefers.'

Kirsty smiled and acquiesced. She wandered off to her kitchen to make the coffee.

✻ ✻ ✻

At the far end of the cottage, adjoining the tiny kitchen, was a very small conservatory where Peter and Kirsty had spent an enjoyable autumn watching their weedy garden grow. They'd bought a small heater so that they could come out here in the winter to enjoy the winter sunshine.

Kirsty placed the warm croissants and cafetière on the wicker coffee table in the conservatory, and sat on the small wicker sofa, her legs curled under her, reading her Kindle, and waiting for Peter and his mum to emerge from upstairs.

It was a small cottage. Upstairs there were two bedrooms and a tiny bathroom. Downstairs, there was a small living room, a kitchen-diner and at the far end, and this little conservatory. Luckily the rental also had a separate garage with loft space, and they'd crammed in as many unwanted childhood and university boxes as they could. It was a squeeze, but Kirsty loved it. She loved the cottage charm, she loved the cosy wood burner, she loved the wonky floors and wobbly walls. To her it was perfect.

Heather waddled into the conservatory, followed by Peter. He fussed over his mum to make sure she had a blanket for her knees and started pouring her a coffee. He poured himself one and sat down heavily next to Kirsty.

Kirsty reached over to the cafetière to pour herself a coffee. Relaxing back into Peter, as he draped his arm around her shoulders, she asked Heather, 'Have you settled in okay? Did Peter manage to get all your bags upstairs?'

Peter answered for his mum. 'The room is a little small, so I've put some of Mum's bags in our room. I knew you wouldn't mind.' He gave her shoulder a little squeeze.

Kirsty replied, 'No, no, not at all. I'm glad you could fit them in.' Smiling she added, 'Heather, we're very glad to have you with us for Christmas.'

Heather corrected her, 'And New Year.' She turned to Peter and said, 'You did mention to Kirsty about New Year too?'

Peter looked surprised, 'I'm sorry, Mum. I didn't know that you wanted to stay for the New Year as well, but of course, it's not a problem. Kirsty and I are glad to have you with us. Aren't we, darling?' He gave her shoulder another squeeze.

Kirsty smiled through her glug of coffee. 'Absolutely, Heather. It's a delight to have you with us.'

Heather sat opposite them, nodding in satisfaction. She added, 'And of course, we have Midnight Mass tonight too. It's not just about the presents you know, it's about a little baby called Jesus being born. Peter used to love going to Midnight Mass when he was a little boy. I go to the church regularly. I'm thinking of becoming a lay person. And I've even toyed with the idea of becoming a vicar.'

Kirsty took another big glug of hot coffee, as Peter replied, 'Oh yes, Midnight Mass. I haven't done that for years. Well, it's very Christmassy, I guess we could go.' He turned his face and raised his eyebrows at Kirsty.

Kirsty nodded in agreement. 'That sounds lovely. Why not?' she said.

* * *

The carols for Midnight Mass started at ten-thirty and by eleven, the service was in full swing. It finished somewhere around midnight. Heather wanted to have a discussion with the vicar afterwards, so they all went to the vicarage for mince pies and mulled wine. Kirsty couldn't drink because she was driving, but she wanted Peter and Heather to enjoy themselves by carrying on Peter's childhood traditions.

The congregation seemed very nice and Peter and Kirsty made small talk as they waited for Peter's mum. People started to thin out and Kirsty noticed that Heather had cornered the vicar, enthralling him with all her charitable works at her local parish.

Peter and Kirsty sat awkwardly at the edge of a table, talking to an old lady who had lost her husband five years before. It was dark outside and cold. Kirsty was feeling tired and tried to disguise a big yawn. The service had been nice, but she just wanted to go home. They had to cook the turkey and Christmas lunch tomorrow and she didn't want them to get it wrong.

As politely as she could, Kirsty tried to indicate to Peter that it was time to go. Eventually, he got the hint, releasing the poor vicar from the corner and ushering his mum to their car.

They finally got back to the cottage at a quarter to one in the morning. Peter's mum insisted that they have their first mince pie of Christmas Day and make a wish, because it was tradition.

Obligingly, Kirsty went to the cupboard and grabbed a couple of mince pies, while Peter poured them all a small glass of sherry. They went through to the cool living room where the fire was barely a whisper, and sitting down ate their mince pie and made a wish. Kirsty's wish was that this would be the year that Peter would finally propose to her, and she could have the life she dreamed of with him.

Kirsty's thoughts were broken by Heather, saying to Peter, 'Our other post-Midnight Mass tradition is that we always open one present. You're forgetting all the important traditions, Peter!'

Peter exclaimed, 'Oh yes, I'd forgotten about that.'

Kirsty tried to disguise a yawn as Heather ferreted underneath the rainbow-flashing Christmas tree, hunting for presents. It was a quarter past one in the morning.

Kirsty had arranged the presents as neatly as she could this afternoon, including the silver-hologram-paper covered presents that Heather had brought with her today. Most of them appeared to be for Peter.

Heather stopped digging in the collapsed pile of presents exclaiming, 'I have one for you Peter, and I have one for you Kirsty! Now let me select one for me.' Going back down the hole she selected a particularly large present for herself. As she pulled it out from underneath the tree, she scattered a few small gifts across the carpet.

Happily, she passed Peter's present to him and passed Kirsty a small, flat, square box.

Kirsty set her sherry down on the coffee table, and sitting on the sofa with Peter, she tried to stay positive saying, 'What a lovely tradition. I'm so glad that you mentioned it. It's not something we've done before is it, Peter?'

Heather dragged her big present into the middle of the room, and started ripping at the red, recyclable, wrapping paper and multicoloured raffia that Kirsty had so carefully decorated it with.

Kirsty turned to her own present. It was from Peter. Carefully undoing the wrapping she found a navy-blue jewellery box. Inside was a gold snake-chain necklace holding a small diamond pendant. Kirsty clamped her hand over her mouth and turned to Peter, saying, 'What a beautiful gift, this must have cost you so much money. I absolutely adore it!'

Peter looked a little embarrassed, 'I'm glad you like it. It's your main gift. I'm sorry you won't have much else to open tomorrow, if that's ok. But I'm glad you like it.'

Kirsty assured him. 'It's a lovely present. It's so thoughtful of you. I really am touched.' and she kissed his cheek.

Heather was so busy, noisily ripping paper away from her present, that she had completely missed Kirsty's beautiful present from her son.

Excitedly, Heather revealed her gift inside. It was a green-and-blue, satin, hand-painted, counterpane. Quite modern and unusual. Heather's face changed, she gave a tight smile and said, 'This will come in very useful tonight to keep me warm.' She made a mock shiver adding, 'Cottages are so cold, aren't they?'

Peter turned to his present. Unwrapping it he found some underwear from his mum. Smiling he said, 'Thanks, Mum. Always useful.'

Heather stated, 'Well I always buy your underwear, don't I?'

Kirsty tried not to yawn, but Peter noticed and suggested that they all head to bed.

Kirsty was the last in the bathroom. She washed off her makeup and slipped into her pyjamas. Checking her phone, it read two a.m. She was shattered. It wasn't the Christmas that she'd been expecting, but she guessed that sometimes you had to adjust.

❉ ❉ ❉

At seven a.m. sharp, Heather clicked up the latch on her wooden bedroom door and noisily descended the wooden stairs to the living room, and on through to the kitchen, where she started to make a fry-up for breakfast.

Groggily, Kirsty ran her hand over her face and eyes before stretching her hand out to her phone to check the time. Groaning internally, she lay her head back against the pillow, and tried to shut out the noise from downstairs.

Peter had also woken up. Sleepily, he ran his arms around Kirsty's body, nuzzling into her neck. He whispered, 'I think a fry-up is just what I need.'

'Aren't you a little tired?' said Kirsty, looking puzzled.

'Yes, I am a bit. But I always have space for a fry-up.'

Giving Kirsty a kiss on her temple, Peter rolled out of bed, pulled his jogging bottoms on over his boxes, and covered his toned torso with an old rugby top from his university days. Reaching for his dressing gown he padded downstairs to be with his mum.

Kirsty tried to shut out the sound of them talking downstairs in the kitchen. She had planned a breakfast of smoked salmon and scrambled eggs on muffins. But if Peter and Heather wanted a fry-up, then it was Christmas, and she wanted them to be happy. Besides they could always have the smoked salmon tomorrow for breakfast. It would keep.

Kirsty felt a bit frustrated. It wasn't exactly the Christmas she had planned, and it was difficult, trying to accommodate somebody else's traditions, but Heather was lonely and Peter was happy to have his mum over. It was up to Kirsty to try and think about everybody else. Lying under the warm duvet, she wondered if she could get away with another half-hour of sleep before she had to get up and play hostess.

✳ ✳ ✳

'You finally made it up then!' Heather said from the conservatory, as Kirsty emerged in her dressing gown, observing her battleground of a kitchen. There were greasy pots and pans everywhere. On the counters were plates, the abandoned half-eaten food on them congealing with fat. Noisily the extractor fan was still whirring away over the oven.

Kirsty popped off the extractor fan and absent-mindedly started scraping bits of unwanted cold breakfast into the bin, as she replied, 'I was a bit tired after Midnight Mass.' Kirsty almost felt like she needed to defend herself so she embellished and added, 'And I had a little bit of a headache, so I decided to have a bit of a lie-in.'

Peter looked at her with concern and said, 'Are you okay, darling? Do you want a paracetamol?'

Heather made a mock laugh from the conservatory and said, 'Sounds like an excuse for too much alcohol more like.' And laughed to herself.

Kirsty smiled wanly as she started to load plates into the dishwasher, saying, 'It was just a glass of sherry. I think I just didn't get enough sleep that's all.'

Heather's voice sharpened, 'Well I'm sorry if our family Christmas traditions put you out.' There was a tinge of annoyance in her voice.

Kirsty and Peter tried to reply together, reassuring her that it was lovely going to Midnight Mass and they'd really enjoyed it. Mollified, Heather allowed herself to be ushered into the living room. Kirsty noticed that Peter and Heather had already opened the champagne that she had been saving for when they opened the Christmas presents. Internally, she said to herself, "It doesn't matter. It is just for this Christmas."

* * *

'We always used to open our presents after lunch.' Heather announced loudly, as they sat in the living room together.

Kirsty had rushed upstairs to get dressed after cleaning up the kitchen, it was nearing ten a.m. and time for presents. She successfully managed to get half a glass of champagne out the bottle before it disappeared. Kirsty shifted a little uncomfortably next to Peter on the sofa, and hoped he would say something. But he didn't.

Kirsty finally said, 'Well, I guess we can wait until after lunch. It doesn't matter to us, does it love?' She turned to Peter for reassurance, but Peter looked up and smiled over at his mum.

Peter said, 'Anything to make you feel at home, Mum. We both want you to have a lovely Christmas.'

Heather wiggled her bottom into the armchair as she made herself comfy. A smile of satisfaction caught her lips. She replied, 'On the subject of lunch, when are we having lunch? I noticed you hadn't started cooking yet, Kirsty?'

Again, Kirsty felt compelled to defend herself as she replied, 'Well, Peter usually does the bird. I prepped all the vegetables and potatoes yesterday.

We were thinking of putting the turkey in ay about eleven and sitting down for lunch at one p.m? If that suits you?'

Heather looked at Peter and addressed him directly, 'You don't have to spend Christmas Day with me if you prefer to be in the kitchen. I see you are a modern man now and you do the cooking. One p.m. seems a little bit late for my pills, but obviously, I'm fitting around you, as you have been so kind to include me in your Christmas.'

Peter looked with concern at his mum. 'Are you sure that's okay for your medication? We're both so happy to have you with us, and I think that it's great we can mix our traditions together to make it work.' Happily, he gave Kirsty a hug.

Kirsty clutched her empty champagne flute and wondered if she should make the kamikaze suggestion of watching a film together until lunchtime. She had the distinct feeling that whatever she suggested wouldn't be quite right.

* * *

After lunch, they sat around with their glasses of wine and opened their presents. Kirsty had had her main present the evening before, so she only had a few little presents of shower gels, hand creams, a mug, and a tin of shortbread biscuits from Heather. Most of the presents were for Peter. Heather was particularly excited by some of what she called, "going out shirts" that she'd bought for him, insisting that he went upstairs and try them on, before commenting on how he should wear the sleeves and how many buttons to have open at the neckline.

Heather turned to Kirsty and said, 'I always think he looks so much better when he has two buttons open and his cuffs rolled up twice, don't you think so?'

Peter looked uncomfortable as he stood in the living room in his jogging bottoms, big, fluffy, wool socks, and Pierre Cardin silk shirt in dark blue.

Kirsty replied, 'Peter is an adult now. I just let him choose whatever he wants to wear. I don't think it's my business to tell him.'

Heather looked as though she'd eaten a lemon, and turning to Peter, she instructed him to go upstairs and change into the green one. Obediently, Peter turned around and padded back up to the bedroom, where he changed shirts and came back down to show it to his mum for her inspection.

❄ ❄ ❄

Kirsty unloaded and loaded the dishwasher, and put all the unwanted Christmas wrapping paper and boxes in the recycling bins out the back alone, while Peter and his mum watched *Songs of Praise* together.

Heather came into the kitchen and said she was thinking about putting together a few pick up snacks for their supper. Heather kindly suggested that Kirsty should put her feet up in the living room, 'My little thank you for putting me up over Christmas.' she said, as she patted Kirsty's arm.

Kirsty joined Peter in the living room and slumped on the sofa as Peter stoked the fire. When he sat next to her, she snuggled into him, wrapping a blanket around them. It was then that she realised they hadn't kissed since Heather had arrived. She suddenly felt very lonely and detached from her physical connection with him. Kirsty wound her arms around his waist under the blanket and brushed her hand against the bulge in his joggers.

Peter smiled down at her, but lifted her arm from his waist and said, 'Hey darling, I love you too, but I don't want Mum to see.' Kirsty felt her heart drop like a lead balloon.

Kirsty was trying very hard to not feel rejected as she cuddled into Peter. She knew it was a small cottage, she didn't know Heather that well, and she hadn't realised the Christmas traditions were so strong in their family. Kirsty tried hard to bite her tongue. She just had to get through these few days without upsetting Peter's mum. This lady was going to be her mother-in-law and it was important that they all got on.

❊ ❊ ❊

Kirsty sat watching the film with Peter, snuggled up in their living room, and she thought she could smell frying smoked salmon. Her heart sunk a little further. Kirsty couldn't help it, she wanted to go out and check. So giving Peter a quick peck on the cheek, she slid out from under the blanket and started to walk towards the kitchen. As she got to the doorway, she heard:

'Oh, she's completely lazy. She didn't even get out of bed until ten a.m. knowing I was staying here! I had to make breakfast for myself and Peter. Plus, I think she drinks quite a lot. She had a hangover and the house is full of wine. Including a very expensive champagne. I don't know how they can afford it. I wonder if she might be one of those gold diggers. And you haven't heard the worst of it.' Heather paused for a fresh intake of breath before continuing her assassination, 'She wore a miniskirt to church! I was so ashamed. I made a comment to the vicar about it, and obviously he was very understanding. . .'

Kirsty's cheeks flamed red. Shame washed down through her body and back up again as she thought back to her attire the evening before. She'd worn a knee-length jumper dress with leggings and flat knee-high boots. She'd also worn a three-quarter-length, wool coat, so unless you undid the coat, it was impossible to see what she was wearing underneath.

Kirsty was mortified. She couldn't believe what Heather was saying about her. Swallowing hard, she robotically turned around and walked back into the living room with Peter, who was laughing at the Christmas film, wrapped up in the blanket, sitting on their sofa. On autopilot, she got under the blanket and snuggled in. She was in shock at Heather's true opinion of her. . .

Heather thought Kirsty was a harlot and an alcoholic gold-digger. Even worse, this was the impression she had gathered in under a day from the way Kirsty had behaved. Kirsty tried to examine her behaviour and think back to all the things that would have given Heather a reason to believe these things about her. Kirsty felt as if her dreams of engagement had been shattered like a mirror being hit with a hammer. If this is what Heather thought of her then there was no way that she'd want them to get engaged. Kirsty could feel all her hopes of marriage slipping away.

* * *

The next morning, Boxing Day, Kirsty wasn't feeling her normal happy self. She slept in a little late again, claiming to Peter she had a headache. He knew she wasn't an alcoholic, but she might as well use the headache excuse to her advantage, as things were decidedly uncomfortable.

When Kirsty finally surfaced, she put on a all-in-one and padded down to the kitchen to grab herself a buttered muffin and sit in the conservatory for five minutes with a cup of tea, and a Christmas story on her Kindle. Peter and his mum were already in the conservatory, and his mum was instructing Peter on what he had to do in the garden.

Kirsty greeted them both. She'd seen the mess of her kitchen as she walked through. It seemed that they'd already had their fry-up.

Kirsty sat down on the small wicker sofa next to Peter. Heather addressed Kirsty directly saying, 'You know all this drinking is going to spoil your pretty looks.'

Kirsty felt like she had to stand up for herself. Politely she said, 'Yes, absolutely. I'll make it my New Year's resolution.' Kirsty obviously swiped up on the screen of her Kindle. She wanted to read her Christmas story, but Heather had other ideas.

'Peter said you were looking to buy a house together next year. I had a look online last night, and I've sent emails this morning to the agents of three houses that I think would suit you very well.' Kirsty looked up, shocked. At least Peter also raised his eyebrows in a modicum of surprise. Heather was going much too far.

Heather continued, 'I've noticed that this cottage is quite draughty, and you don't want an old house like this as you'll be spending all your money maintaining it, so I found some nice modern houses.'

Kirsty was horrified. She hated modern houses; they were so tiny and soulless. It really wasn't her idea of their first house together at all. Kirsty turned to Peter for support, she reached out her hand, and nuzzled it inside his hand, squeezing it, hoping that he would understand.

Instead, Peter said, 'Thanks, Mum, that's really kind. We will have a look at your house bookings later, won't we darling?' He turned to Kirsty with a smile on his face.

Kirsty felt cold. Everything she thought she knew about Peter was slipping away, as she discovered a spineless side to him; one that let his mum walk all over them. He seemed to have no thought for how Kirsty felt. They hadn't kissed in two days because he was worried that his mum might hear. Kirsty was starting to feel like the gooseberry in their relationship.

Kirsty swallowed hard, but the words wouldn't come out. So, Peter tried to encourage an answer out of her by taking her hand and reiterated, 'Won't we darling?'

Kirsty was just about able to manage a smile before Heather continued to bulldoze the conversation. 'Well, if you go with one of my suggestions, I will contribute ten thousand pounds to your deposit.' She folded her hands on her lap and closed her eyes graciously at her own goodness. 'I did the same for your brother, and I will do the same for you.'

Peter excitedly said, 'That's so generous. We really appreciate it. Don't we Kirsty?' and again he tugged on her hand, trying to pull an answer out of her. All Kirsty could think was that this was ten thousand pounds of Heather dominating their house selection and inviting herself over whenever she wanted. This was *not* what Kirsty had planned for her life together with Peter. Her hopes of a happy married life with the person she loved slipped away.

* * *

Kirsty spent Boxing Day tidying up behind Peter and Heather. When *they* wanted to go out for a walk, she just sat quietly in the conservatory, and let them go. She tried to read her Kindle, but she couldn't focus. Kirsty felt cold and lonely. She was questioning everything. Two days ago, she thought she would be engaged by New Year. Now she was questioning if she would say "Yes."

Kirsty felt like Peter's mum was another woman in their relationship, worse than that, his mum was the woman who took priority. If this was the way the dynamics were settling now, this was the way it was always going to be. Kirsty could either accept Peter for allowing his mum to intrude on their relationship and dominate their life, because she loved him, or she could be brave and walk away, seeing this as a notch in her relationship experiences.

Big, fat tears started to roll down Kirsty's cheeks, and she stifled a sob. In the lane outside the little cottage, she could hear Peter and his mum walking back towards the cottage. Quickly, Kirsty turned off her Kindle and rushed upstairs to slip under the duvet cover in their bedroom and tried to stop crying.

* * *

That night, Peter snuggled into bed next to Kirsty and wrapped his arms around her. He sensed something wasn't quite right. Kirsty had had a headache over dinner and hadn't eaten that much.

Gently, Peter asked, 'Are you okay, darling?'

Kirsty spoke to the darkness, 'Yes, I'm okay, just a bit headachy that's all. I think I've just been over-doing it a little bit this Christmas.'

Accepting her reply, Peter gave her a kiss on the back of her head and rolled over. Within a few minutes, he was snoring. Kirsty lay still in the darkness, as cold, fat tears rolled down her cheeks onto her pillow, making it wet and chilling the side of her cheek as the wet patch spread.

* * *

Heather wanted to stay until New Year and Kirsty didn't know how much more of this she could take. Kirsty had taken to wearing trousers and big, baggy jumpers, because she didn't want to be accused of dressing inappropriately. Even though she knew that it wasn't true, the comments still stung. When Peter offered her a glass of wine with the evening meal, she hesitated. This was ridiculous. Kirsty was in her home, being offered wine that she'd bought and felt unable to drink it.

After dinner, they decided to go through to the living room and watch another Christmas film.

Peter found the film *Trolls* on the TV guide. He knew that Kirsty loved the film. Within ten minutes Heather started making disparaging comments in her corner armchair and waddled out to the kitchen to phone Peter's brother instead.

Peter offered to get Kirsty a drink. Kirsty opted for tea and Peter followed his mum out. He came back with Kirsty's tea and handed it to her with a scowl. Kirsty noticed and said, 'Are you okay, love? Is everything okay?' Peter sat down carefully next to her and pulling the blanket over his lap, he wrapped his arm around her, gave her a squeeze and kissed the side of her head, 'Yeah, everything is fine.'

Heather spent the evening in the conservatory, with the little heater, talking to her friends. Throughout the film, Peter didn't say a word.

✻ ✻ ✻

The next morning Kirsty got to work clearing away the greasy pots and pans from Heather's fried breakfast.

Peter squeezed her shoulder and said, 'Let me give you a hand with that.'

Kirsty was surprised, because for the last few days she seemed to be the only one that noticed the mess, as Peter and his mum moved from activity to activity. Gratefully Kirsty smiled and said, 'Thank you'.

Kirsty stood up from the dishwasher and Peter handed her another plate, as he did so he looked at the tender space at the base of her neck and said, 'That necklace looks beautiful on you. I'm so glad that you like it.'

Absentmindedly, Kirsty touched the necklace and said, 'I love it. It's a beautiful Christmas gift.' Their eyes connected and they basked in each other's gaze. For the first time in days, Kirsty felt bonded to him.

* * *

Peter's mum suggested they visit a garden centre for lunch. Relieved to not have to clean up her kitchen again, Kirsty wholeheartedly agreed. Perhaps she could get herself lost amongst the poinsettias and potted orchids, or even go to the aquarium area and have a look at the fish. She started to cheer up a little.

Peter's mum ordered the steak and chips, she also wanted pudding and had two large glasses of wine. Naturally, Peter offered to pick up the bill, but it was eating into their house deposit savings. At home, Heather had worked her way through half their wine store. Kirsty kept to lemonade over lunch, she was terrified of being branded an alcoholic. It was silly. She wasn't. The source of her uncertainty was because she wasn't confident in her relationship with Peter anymore.

After lunch, they walked around the garden centre. Heather selected some plants that she wanted to take home with her. When they got to the checkout, Heather suddenly realised that she'd left her purse back at their little cottage, so graciously, Peter offered to pay.

Kirsty couldn't help the thought popping into her head; she wondered if Heather had purposely forgotten it. Kirsty had been trying to not to let Heather's comments upset her, and in a small act of rebellion, she'd worn the same jumper dress that she'd worn on Christmas Eve to Midnight Mass.

The fact was not lost on Heather. When they stopped mid-afternoon for a cup of coffee in the conservatory, Heather made a comment to Peter about Kirsty, saying, 'I'm quite surprised that you went for a blonde.' Nodding in the direction of Kirsty, but not looking at her. 'Blondes aren't your type at all. You've only ever been attracted to brunettes.'

The comment hung heavily in the air. Peter just shrugged and gave Kirsty a hug around her shoulders saying, 'Kirsty is just special I guess.' Looking down, he gave her a kind smile. It seemed like this was the first time that Peter had stood up for her all week.

But Heather wasn't finished. Continuing she said, 'And she wears such short dresses. Your dad always found it quite incredible when he picked you up from nightclubs; seeing the tiny bits of cloth women wore. Yes, you're right, Kirsty doesn't seem like your type at all.'

Kirsty felt Peter tense as he said, 'I think Kirsty dresses really nicely, and she's perfect for me just the way she is.'

Heather couldn't miss the opportunity to drive her point home, as she retorted, 'Oh well, I guess it's your choice.'

Peter sat a little straighter, his foot started rhythmically twitching. 'Yes, actually, it is my choice, and I choose Kirsty. I'm really sorry that you have a problem with that, Mum.'

Heather laughed dismissively at the comment, 'I don't have a problem with that. Silly boy.'

Peter's foot started twitching even more as he said, 'I'm not a silly boy, Mum, and I heard what you were saying to my brother on the phone last night. I don't appreciate you making comments like that about Kirsty actually. I think it might be a good idea if you went and spent New Year with my brother.'

Kirsty sat open-mouthed, looking from Peter to Heather, and Heather to Peter. Her cheeks flamed red with the shame of what she guessed Heather had said about her, and what Peter had heard. Kirsty was mortified and she felt ashamed for who she was, and how she looked.

Looking down at her lap, Kirsty found some small bobbles on her jumper dress and tried to remove them carefully. She could feel her eyes welling up with tears, inside her heart, she was overwhelmed that Peter was finally standing up for her. Kirsty felt so awkward that she didn't know what to do or say.

Heather took the lead, as she burst out crying, saying, 'I don't know what I've done to upset you both. I've tried so hard, but I've consistently been made to feel unwelcome.' She pointed at Kirsty. 'That woman's changed you. You know, Peter, you're not the same loving boy you used to be.'

Peter exploded. 'I've had enough, Mum. I love you, but I think it's time you left.'

Hysterically sobbing, Peter's mum stood up, screaming, 'Fine. I will leave. I know where I'm not wanted.'

Kirsty felt like she should say something, but she didn't know what to say. This was equally Peter's house too, and he knew best how to deal with his mum. Kirsty felt like anything she said now would be used against her, so she stayed looking down at her dress, trying to remove small bobbles of fluff.

Peter stood up, replying, 'That's not a problem. Let me help you pack.' He walked out of the conservatory and walked off upstairs. Heather took one look at Kirsty's bowed head and said to herself, 'I wish I'd never come to this twisted place.'

* * *

Kirsty stayed in the conservatory until she heard the front door slam and Peter's mum drive up the road.

A calm started to descend on the house. Kirsty heard Peter come into the kitchen and flick the kettle on for a cup of tea. Making the tea, he brought in a mug for them both, and quietly sat down next to Kirsty. He rested his head back on the wicker sofa and took a deep breath before taking a sip of hot tea. Then he reached out and grabbed Kirsty's hand. Her head was bowed, so he couldn't see the tears that were streaming down her face.

Eventually, he turned to look at her saying, 'I'm so sorry that my mum said those things about you. I don't know why she's behaved this way. Perhaps she's lonely. But I don't want you to think I don't love you or I won't stand up for you. I really appreciate how accommodating you've been this last week; I know it must have been hard on you.'

Kirsty raised her tear-stained face to his, and it was only then that he realised she'd been crying. His face fell, and he reached out his hand as he tried to wipe the tears away from her hot cheeks, saying, 'I'm so sorry, I don't want you upset like this, on our first Christmas living together.'

Kirsty didn't have the words, so she just shook her head and tried to sniff back the tears. Eventually, she managed to say, 'But she's your mum, Peter, and she hates me. What are we going to do now?'

Peter looked confidently down at her, and giving her shoulders a big squeeze, he kissed her on top of her head and said, 'I know exactly what to do. I don't want you to worry about it, okay?'

Kirsty sadly nodded. Tears continued to streak down her face and she buried her head into Peter's secure chest.

* * *

The cottage started to feel like home again. Kirsty still found that she hesitated when Peter offered her a glass of wine, and she scrutinised her clothes in the mirror each morning in case they came up too short or too low. She hated this. She didn't want to feel this way about herself. The last week had also been a shock regarding her relationship with Peter. She'd felt like he had abandoned her, and although he stood up for her in the end, she had to consider the fact that his mum would always be in his life. Kirsty found herself questioning everything, even her choice of job and whether she was earning enough. The comment about her being a gold digger still stung.

It was New Year's Eve and Peter tried to make the evening as nice as possible. He cooked them a curry and tidied up all by himself, insisting that he was going to load the dishwasher. He bought a replacement bottle of champagne and they shared it. They spent the evening snuggled up on the sofa, in front of the rainbow-coloured sparkling Christmas tree and cosy wood burner.

Peter sweetly went through some photos of their relationship together, that he'd arranged in an album on his iPad. Kirsty started to remember all the wonderful times that they'd had. She remembered how nice it felt being around him, how easily they talked and how similar they were. She found her heart started to melt; she knew she loved Peter more than anything. Life was complicated. Could Peter be the one that Kirsty could make a marriage with?

Watching the fireworks in London on the TV, they cheered in the New Year. Clinking champagne flutes together, they took a sip and their eyes connected. Peter carefully reached out for Kirsty's flute and placed both of them on the coffee table. He got up from the sofa and knelt in front of her. Taking both of her hands in his, he said:

'From the moment I met you at my friend's party, I knew you were the one. Since then, there has never been another woman who can come close to you. I want you to know that you're the one for me, Kirsty. You're kind and you're beautiful. You're intelligent and you're sweet. Please do me the honour of becoming my wife?'

Peter reached his hand under a cushion on the sofa, and brought out a small, red box. Inside was a small, diamond solitaire, gold ring.

Kirsty started shaking, she couldn't help it. She felt like she'd been through so much the last week. She'd questioned everything, but having their little home back to themselves, looking through the photographs of their relationship, and remembering all the things that made them special, Kirsty, in her heart of hearts, knew Peter was the one for her. She appreciated they would have their ups and downs, but Peter had shown he would stand up for her, and she knew she had a good man by her side.

Kirsty nodded, and looking Peter in the eyes, she said, 'Yes.' Before bursting into tears.

Peter wrapped her in his arms and her tears turned to laugher and happiness. Peter looked down at her, and lowering his head to hers, their lips connected, sensitively, in a kiss.

7.   ELF LOVE

In a sleepy, suburban part of town, some large, white, wooden-boarded detached houses sat conversationally arranged around each other. Their white picket fences demarking their perfectly manicured gardens and neat, pretty shrubs. All except one house. Near the centre of the development. The house where old Mrs Verdrain lived.

Mrs Verdrain had moved into the house, with her husband, over fifteen years ago. It was to be their forever home to see them out; their high point after a long life of working. And they'd had ten good years together in their beautiful home until, sadly, Mr Verdrain contracted cancer five years ago and the lifelong soulmates were finally parted.

Mrs Verdrain was a stoic sort of person so she tried to make the best of it and stay busy, as best she could.

Mrs Verdrain had white, curly hair and a kindly demeanour. Although she didn't have the energy or the money to keep the garden quite as nicely as all her neighbours, she did very well at keeping herself busy by taking delight in entertaining all the neighbourhood children; often sitting on her porch to talk with them during the warm summer days. When it came to winter, she found that she was a little lonelier without her dear husband, however, the children adored her and kept her company. They would often pop by to her house in their twos and threes, to sit by her fire and listen to her stories. And so it was, two neighbourhood children, Timothy and Sabina, visited Mrs Verdrain with a homemade chicken pie that Timothy's mum had cooked for her.

Mrs Verdrain was delighted to see the children and helped them off with their snow boots and puffy coats. She hung their scarves up on the coat hooks in the hall with her shaky, bruised hands; made them glasses of orange squash and got them some cookies; and sat down in her favourite chair by the fire, next to them, to knit and tell them stories. It was a ritual which delighted them all.

Mrs Verdrain asked, 'So, my darlings, have you written your letters to Santa? Have you been good children this year? What gifts have you asked for?'

Sabina excitedly replied, 'I've been very good this year. I've helped Mummy in the kitchen and I've helped Daddy in the garden, and I've even looked after my little brother when he was very annoying. I've asked Santa for a Barbie doll with a caravan, so that she can go away on a holiday. I really hope Santa remembers.'

Timothy interrupted, 'And I've been very good too. I even helped roll out the pastry for your chicken pie.' Mrs Verdrain raised her eyebrows in appreciation and encouragement. Timothy continued, 'I always take my muddy boots off before coming into the house, and I clear out my hamster cage before Mum even asks me to. I've been very good this year. I've asked Santa for a new bike.' Timothy nodded his head in full expectation that his request would be answered. This was transactional. It was pretty clear: If you were good then Santa delivered presents. That's how it worked.

'Well,' Mrs Verdrain said significantly, 'You know how Santa watches you, to know if you've been naughty or nice, don't you?'

Both the children looked stupefied and shook their heads, "No."

'You don't?' Mrs Verdrain smiled and paused her knitting for a second as she said, 'It's the elves. Santa's elves leave the North Pole to go and check on all the little girls and boys, to make sure that they've been good. Perhaps if you haven't seen any elves then Santa won't know.' Mrs Verdrain smiled and winked as her knitting needles started to *click-clack* again.

Sabina looked concerned, 'Oh, Mrs Verdrain, I've not seen any elves. Maybe Santa doesn't know that I've been a good girl this year, and I won't get my Barbie with a camper van after all!' Sabina looked panicked, and Timothy's eyebrows knitted together in concern.

Mrs Verdrain smiled broadly at them and said, 'Well, my darlings, I have the perfect solution. I will knit you an elf each. You can sit them in your bedrooms and they can watch all the good things you do. Then Santa will know that you are good children. How does that sound?'

Sabina and Timothy smiled. They thought that sounded like an excellent idea.

* * *

The rooves of the large, white-wood houses were thick with snow, and little chimney stacks scaled up the sides of the homes to release curly, grey waves of smoke; to show that all was well and warm within. The windows glowed with yellowy lights and were adorned with green foliage wreaths. There were also large foliage wreaths on the doors, beckoning in the Christmas season. Each house had at least one sparkling Christmas tree, stood sentry at a window to give pleasure to all, inside and out, should you take a moment to stop and admire them.

True to her word, Mrs Verdrain knitted two special little elves for Sabina and Timothy, one girl elf and one boy elf respectively. But she hadn't used just any old wool, she'd unwound some of the wool from her late husband's jumpers and an old one of hers that she no longer used, to give the right shades of reds and greens, whites and pinks. She gave the elves little, pink, knitted faces; tiny button eyes; and removable mittens and coats to keep them warm from the cold weather outside.

Sabina and Timothy were delighted with their elves and sat them pride of place in their bedrooms. When the children went to bed that night, each of them reminded the little elves to tell Santa how good they'd been, and to make sure that Santa definitely knew to deliver them presents this year.

❄ ❄ ❄

It was the dead of night, and in Sabina's quiet house, the antique grandfather clock in the hall chimed twelve. The house was dark and still. Little flurries of snow continued to fall outside. The Christmas tree sat lit in then front window was sparkling out its fairy light onto the deserted street. The wide glass doors at the back of the house looked out onto the covered pool in the back garden, and beyond the white fence was the back of Timothy's house.

Stretching her little woollen arms, the elf delicately lowered herself from the shelf in the bedroom and wondered how long she had been sleeping for. She had the distinct feeling that she needed to meet someone. She wasn't quite sure where she was, or where she was going, but she knew that staying on the shelf wasn't the right thing to do. Carefully she slipped through the gap in the door; Sabina's mum had thoughtfully placed a little doorstop toy there to wedge the door open and allow the landing light to filter into Sabina's bedroom while she slept.

Carefully guiding herself down the stairs, the elf stood at the base of the stairs to the open-plan living area and gazed at the sparkling Christmas tree. She didn't think she'd ever seen anything quite so amazing before.

Walking up to the tree she could see clearly the little, warm-white, twinkling icicle lights. She reached out a little, woolly hand and touched them as if they contained some kind of magic. The tree was adorned with little silver baubles and delicate wooden snowflake shapes painted white. She could have looked at it for ages, but she knew she had to be going.

Just as she turned her back to leave, she noticed a lady sat on top of the tree. Remembering her manners, she called out, 'Hello? Hello? Are you okay up there?' But the lady on top of the tree remained silent and didn't even acknowledge her. Perhaps she was just sleeping? Shrugging her shoulders, the elf turned away from the tree and made her way to the back of the house.

At the far end of the kitchen were two glass doors, looking out onto the snow-covered back garden. There was a white-wood house the other side of the fence. The elf looked out of the glass doors, placing her little woolly hands on the glass, as she pressed her face close to it and started searching for something.

Snow was falling in swirls and eddies. Little snow drifts had caught against the bushes making scooped meringue shapes. The elf wasn't quite sure what she was searching for, so she let her eyes roam and looked as far as she could see.

The elf had nearly given up, to go back to sleep on her shelf, when there in the distance she thought she saw a movement in an upstairs window. Straining her eyes hard, she looked again. Yes, there it was, a very small person just like her, pressed against the window and waving. She waved back.

They couldn't really talk to each other, so they just stood there for a while looking at each other, waving to the other elf that looked just like them: the same little knitted green and red jackets, the same little pink hands, the same little, green, pointy hats. The elf felt quite sure that this was who she was looking for. Her heart breathed a sigh of relief. She wasn't alone.

* * *

It was desperately sad. The very next morning Mrs Wickham from across the road, knocked on Mrs Verdrain's door to deliver some freshly made minestrone soup, and found that she couldn't get an answer. She was quite concerned so she called the emergency services. Within twenty minutes they'd arrived, gained entry, and confirmed what the worried crowd of neighbours gathering had feared. Mrs Verdrain had passed away in the night.

Mrs Verdrain was found in her bed, clutching a silver framed black-and-white photo of her wedding day. In the photo she stood with her late husband, in front of a tiny, white chapel. They were young and beautiful. They were happy, with their whole lives stretched out ahead of them on the advent of adventure. They were in love.

It seemed that Mrs Verdrain had been very short of money and she hadn't been heating her house properly. The cold combined with old age (and possibly a lonely heart) meant that her body had decided it was time to go. One of the neighbours remembered that she had a nephew living in a city a few hundred miles south, and the authorities worked to try and establish next of kin; to ensure Mrs Verdrain would be given a proper funeral.

Sabina and Timothy cherished their little elves even more, now that they knew it was the last gift from their long-time friend. Timothy decided that he was going to call his elf Noel because Noel meant Christmas. Sabina thought it was a good idea, so she called her elf Holly.

Sabina sat in Timothy's kitchen, eating warm buttered tea cakes, while their parents discussed some of the arrangements regarding Mrs Verdrain's funeral. The children talked in whispers, as they drank their milk and ate their tea cakes.

Whispering, Timothy said, 'Something strange happened last night.' he looked at Sabina significantly.

'What was it?' Sabina asked.

'My elf, Noel. I put him at the end of my bed when I went to sleep. But when I woke up, he was by the window, just like he was looking out.'

'Perhaps your mum came in and moved him?'

'Perhaps.'

Then Sabina added flippantly, 'Perhaps he just wanted to look out the window?'

Timothy nodded. Perhaps he did just want to look out the window. It must be hard being a stuffed toy; quite a boring life really. Timothy decided that he'd leave some elf sized clothes and food for Noel when he went to bed tonight, so that he wouldn't be quite so bored.

❈ ❈ ❈

Noel woke up to find he was in a small bed (borrowed from Timothy's sister's Barbie collection) at the end of Timothy's bed. Beside him was a small plastic Barbie car, some miniature sandwiches, some small slices of apple and a scarf borrowed from a teddy bear.

Noel was quite surprised. He'd never eaten human food before; he wasn't exactly sure how. He had a go, but he just got pâté and breadcrumbs over his little, pink, woolly face, so he gave up. Besides, he wanted to see if his friend was at the window again tonight. He wanted to wave to her.

Carefully lowering himself down from the bed, Noel made his way over to the window. Clambering up, he pressed his face to the glass. He could see the neighbour's garden covered with snow. The large glass doors emanated a dull twinkling glow from within. Noel strained his eyes to see if he could see his friend. Perhaps she wasn't there tonight. He looked again. Yes! There she was. A little, wobbly shadow coming into view, she pressed her face and hands against the glass, and spotting him, waved.

Just like last night he waved back, and even though they were miles apart, he felt as if he could almost see into her eyes.

❄ ❄ ❄

The very next night, Noel decided that he *had* to meet her. Bravely he took a wipe of his cheese sandwich for nourishment, lowered the Barbie car down from the bed and drove it to the top of the stairs.

Noel perched at the top of the stairs and peered down. Taking a deep breath, he drove forward. It was a bit of a bumpy ride, and the last bump at the bottom of the stairs had been quite a shock; it catapulted him straight out of the car, towards the back door, out the cat flap, and on into the freezing snow.

Noel lifted his little face out from the snow drift and tried to puff the snowflakes away. Nothing broken. Nonplussed he stood up, pulled his little jacket tighter around him and donned his mittens. He then started the journey across the garden and over the fence to meet his friend.

When Noel reached the window, she wasn't there, but he didn't have to wait long. Within minutes, Holly appeared at the window smiling.

She pressed her face to the glass; her little hands raised up either side, looking out at him.

Noel wondered if they also had a catflap and walked around the side of the house to see. He was in luck! He carefully poked his torso inside the flap but losing his balance he somersaulted into the kitchen. Noel's feet and legs were wet with the snow and his body was shivering, but his heart was warm.

Holly stood in front of him. Glancing up he couldn't take his eyes off her. She wore a cute little red dress with white snowflakes along the hem and a little green-and-red jacket just like him. Her hair was scooped up in little blonde bunches at the sides of her head; she had a little pointy, green hat with a bell on the end; and little pointy ears. Noel felt like he'd met his other half, his soul mate.

It was clear that Holly felt the same way about Noel. She rushed towards him saying, 'Oh my goodness! You must be so cold and wet. Do come in by the fire and warm yourself.'

Hand in hand they wobbled over to the fire and sat down on the furry mat. Comfortably they introduced themselves, and talked and laughed until the light started to lift outside the window, and Noel said he really must go.

❋ ❋ ❋

For the next few nights, Noel would come to visit Holly, sit by the fire, and talk to her. Sometimes the cat came in and gave them a suspicious look, but left them alone. Sometimes, Noel would bring some tiny sandwiches or pieces of apple that Timothy left, not that they could eat it, but at least he felt like he was bringing something to her. The garden was bereft of flowers and covered in snow. If Noel could have found flowers, he would have given them all to her.

It was on Christmas Eve that Noel hatched his plan. He had ventured into Timothy's sister's bedroom, and in her doll's jewellery box he found a large plastic ring, big enough to go around Holly's wrist. Noel was sure that Timothy and his sister wouldn't mind him taking it, if they knew what he had planned.

When Noel popped through the catflap that evening, he tried to hide the ring behind him. Taking Holly's hand, he led her over to the Christmas tree and under the twinkling icicle lights and little white snowflakes, Noel asked Holly to marry him. Of course, she said, "Yes".

Excitedly they started to discuss when and where they would get married. They couldn't wait to start their new life together.

Holly was worried, she had heard Sabina's mother talking this afternoon. She wanted to take the Christmas decorations down after Christmas and mentioned boxes and the attic. Holly had a horrible feeling that this might mean that she was going to be put in a box and she wouldn't be able to see Noel anymore.

Noel sat quietly by the fire, looking grave, as he tried to think of a plan. Finally, just before dawn, he said, 'I think I have it. Be ready, tomorrow night. I'm going to take you with me, we're going to elope and we'll find a little chapel, get married, and start a new life together.' His face glowed with happiness in the last glowing embers of the fire. Holding her hands he asked, 'How does that sound?' His excited eyes rested in Holly's, never doubting her for a moment.

Holly replied, 'My love, I will follow you to the moon and back. I can't imagine anything or anywhere I want to be more, than with you.'

Noel smiled contentedly, 'Be ready, tomorrow night, by the catflap. Tomorrow, we elope.'

Tenderly they kissed.

* * *

The very next night the two elves eloped. Holly had never left the house before, but Noel was quite brave. Although he hadn't left the confines of the gardens, he'd taken the opportunity during the day to have a good look around from Timothy's bedroom window, and thought he could probably navigate their way to the end of the street.

Holding Holly's hand and looking braver than he felt, Noel walked them away from the comfort of their homes, and the looming Christmas decoration boxes, out into the dark night and freedom.

The two little elves made good progress. By hiding in park bushes during the day and stowing away on a bus at night, they were able to move to a new city. No one would recognise them here and no one would miss them.

Holly and Noel spent the evening in a city park, sitting on a far-flung bench, away from prying eyes. They held hands as they gazed over the park, listening to a band and enjoying the Christmas lights. Noel suggested that tomorrow they should look for a chapel and get married. Holly kissed his cheek and he wrapped his arms around her. Later they climbed one of the park trees and cuddled up together.

Early the next morning, Noel and Holly walked along the quiet, snowy pavements and found a beautiful little white chapel. It almost felt as if they'd been here before. They mounted the steps of the chapel in the early morning light, and by standing on Holly's shoulders, Noel tried to open the door, but the handle was too high.

Noel was rather good at getting himself into buildings, he wasn't defeated yet. Holding Holly's hand, they walked around the back of the building until he found a back door with a very low letter-box. Noel sized up Holly's slim frame. He was fairly sure that they could manage to get in.

It was a bit of a squeeze, but by holding in their breath, they were able to get through the letter-box. Noel was worried there might be a service today, so they hid behind a floppy-looking display of flowers and waited until they had the chapel to themselves.

* * *

That evening the couple were married.

Noel had found a little white napkin which was the perfect size for Holly's wedding dress. She looked beautiful, whereas he looked a bedraggled mess. He was lucky she took him just the way he was. They stood before the altar to say their vows; promising to love each other forever and to mend each other's stitches.

Unfortunately, the day after they got married, when they were snuggled up together and dozing behind a drooping flower display, the flower lady came in. Noel, in his green outfit, merged into the display, but Holly, in her white wedding dress, looked just like a little doll.

The flower lady picked Holly up and said, 'Oh my goodness. Dear little doll. Who lost you?' She put Holly in her handbag and chucked the old flowers into the bin on her way out of the chapel.

There was nothing Noel could do. He managed to push up the bin lid and tried to scramble after them. The flower lady opened the boot of her car and put her handbag in. The last thing Holly heard was Noel running down the pavement shouting:

'I will find you. Wherever you go. I will find you.' Before the boot slammed shut.

* * *

Noel was miserable without Holly. Fate was so cruel. It gave him the most perfect companion, his other half, the other part of him; and then took her away suddenly, to somewhere he didn't know.

Noel tried to logic it out. The flower lady that had taken Holly must work at the chapel, therefore she must attend the services. He only had to wait until Sunday, spot the same lady again, and sneak into her bag, and she would take him home.

Noel caught a waft of his dirty, smelly wool, stained with muddy slush and crystalising road salt. If this plan was to work, then he needed to have a bath. Hopefully, he wouldn't shrink.

Noel lowered himself into the sink at the back of the chapel. *Brrr*, the water was freezing! Noel scrubbed himself clean with soap, dunked his head under the water and wrung out his body as best he could. In the dim light of the chapel, he sat, cold and wet, waiting for his body to dry.

His plan had to work. Without Holly, life was meaningless.

✳ ✳ ✳

Noel was a clever little elf. That Sunday the flower lady came back to the little white chapel. While she said her prayers and took part in the service, Noel surreptitiously ducked under pews and shimmied underneath the knee rests, until he managed to scramble into the flower lady's bag. He put some tissues over his head to hide himself. His heart beat faster as he waited for her to take him home to Holly.

It was an agonising wait. The flower lady decided to go for a coffee after the service and talked for ages.

Eventually, she got in her car to drive home and debated stopping for some groceries. Thankfully, she decided not to. Minutes felt like hours. All Noel could think about was seeing Holly again.

The flower lady entered her little house and placed her handbag on a hook by the door. She carefully locked the door behind her and went into the kitchen to boil a kettle of water.

Noel carefully lowered himself down from the hanging bag, and dropped to the floor, quickly hiding amongst the boots. Waiting.

* * *

The light faded and Noel heard the flower lady climb the stairs for bed. Peering out of a boot, he looked around. Cautiously exploring the downstairs of the house, he whispered, 'Holly? Holly? Where are you, my love?' Once or twice, he thought he heard a muffled reply, but he couldn't be sure.

Once Noel had searched the ground floor he went upstairs to the bedrooms. Two bedroom doors were closed, and he assumed one belonged to the flower lady. Perhaps Holly was being held captive in the other one? But which door should he choose?

Noel stood still and tried to let his heart guide him. He decided to try the door to his right. Turning, he walked to it, jumped up and looped his woolly arms around the handle. After a few attempts, he managed to spring open the door.

Inside was a little girl's room, but the bed was empty. At the base of the bed was a toy chest with a closed lid. Inside the muffled cries sounded louder.

Noel rushed to the chest, but his little woolly arms couldn't open the lid. He looked around desperately and saw a walking stick with a flapping penguin toy attached. Wedging the stick, he prised open the lid enough for somebody small to crawl out.

Two button eyes blinked at him from the darkness, and a small, pink, woolly hand poked out, and another, then a little green pointy hat with a bell on the end. Holly! His beautiful, beloved wife. Noel helped her out and they hugged tightly.

Noel gasped, 'Oh my love, I'm so sorry, I didn't mean to lead you into danger. I should have been more careful at the chapel. Can you forgive me?'

Holly looked deeply into his eyes and said, 'I have no world without you. There is no need to talk of forgiveness. Only tell me that we will always be together, and I will be happy.'

Gently, Noel kissed her forehead and said, 'I promise my love, whatever happens, we will always be together. Hold my hand and come with me. We're going to escape and start a new life together.'

* * *

On a dark night, somewhere between Christmas and New year, the wobbly silhouettes of two little elves disappeared into a star-lit, snowy night. Engrossed in each other as if no one else in the world existed, or ever could exist.

8. CHRISTMAS PHOTOGRAPHS

Beverly held her camera still as another little child clambered onto Santa's lap and gave him a cuddle.

Snap, snap, snap.

Beverly loved taking photographs at Christmas because people were relaxed and happy and that always gave the best pictures.

The grotto was full of children, and a long line of kids were excitedly waiting to see Santa. Checking her viewfinder, Beverly confirmed the picture quality, and the little child was ushered out for another child to be brought in. It was a long day, even so, Beverly always did the grotto shoots for free. She considered it her duty, because when you have a gift that you can use to contribute to society, then contribute. It was what you were made to do.

Beverly was married to her work. She loved being a photographer. She'd been a photographer all her life, and she couldn't imagine ever retiring (retiring from what? Life?) although some of her friends encouraged her to do so – Beverly just ignored them.

Beverly got home late to her penthouse apartment and pinged herself something to eat in the microwave. She had a few missed calls on her phone, and she carefully selected who she was going to ring back today, while forking hot korma into her mouth. She selected her long-time friend, Marie.

Marie scolded her, 'Darling, are you still doing those grotto shoots with those children.'

Beverly replied, 'You know I am.' She smiled as she knew exactly what Marie was going to say next.

'But darling, do they actually wash? And they're always eating sweets, I mean the sticky just goes everywhere.'

'Oh, I'm so sorry, the line's bad. I can't hear you.'

'Don't hang up on me before you hear what I've got to say! Jeremy has just bought a new gallery and he's looking for an exhibition to kick things off, and we thought it would be wonderful if we could do a display of your life works. What do you think?'

'My life works? I'm not exactly dead yet.'

'No, but you could retire if you wanted to.'

'This isn't a job. This *is* me. This is what I get up for in the morning and what I breathe for every day. Why would I ever retire?'

'Well, exactly darling. So that's why the opening exhibition just has to be yours. Do say yes.'

Beverly smiled. It would be a lot of work, but of course she'd do it. 'Yes.' she replied.

'Fabulous. By the way, it's in two weeks' time, Christmas Eve, don't be late darling.' Marie hung up, and Beverly shook her head at her long-time friend.

* * *

It was quite a rush getting everything printed and framed in time, but somehow, with Marie's help, they managed to get it done.

It was the afternoon of Christmas Eve. Beverly placed her curling tongs back on her dressing table and fluffed the top and back of her silvery-grey hair. Beverly was taller than average with an average figure and long features. She had kind, dark-grey eyes, which twinkled around people. Slipping into her floor-length, purple-velvet mandarin coat, she grabbed her favourite dark-green snakeskin bag, and went downstairs to grab a taxi to the gallery.

Beverly, Marie and Jeremy still had two hours before the exhibition opened. There was barely enough time to make the final touches on the placement of Beverly's photographs to ensure the flow of her exhibition worked. Beverly was a perfectionist in everything she did.

Jeremy and Marie were delighted. Not only did they have the coup of a famous, award-winning photographer, but they'd also sold out all their charity tickets for tonight and were assured of his new venture being a great success. Beverly had insisted the charity was for disadvantaged children's Christmas presents and donated her fees.

The doors opened at seven-thirty p.m. exactly. Excited attendees came to meet the photographer and talk with her, in person, about her pictures. Beverly spent several hours having deep and interesting conversations about perspective, choice of colour, subject selection, and different moods that had taken her through different periods of her life. Her photography had developed over the years, just as she had. There were a lot of questions about her most recent work and where she was going next. Beverly was flattered.

Beverly was particularly gifted at photographing groups of people, where people seemed to be natural and unaware she was there. She was also great at portraits and family groups. She had to be. This was where her main income came from. But it was normal, everyday people, doing normal, everyday things, that she really loved, and it showed in her work.

There were photographs of old men, sitting on benches and talking. Ladies gossiping at the hairdressers. Children swapping toys in the corner of the playground. Farmers taking a break in the shade of a tree and sharing their lunch together. Beverly loved watching people and recording them forever in her photographs.

A younger couple approached Beverly with their two teenage children in tow. It was getting late and Beverly sensed (even though she'd never had children of her own) that they were starting to get a little "bored". The couple enquired about a family shoot, and Beverly was more than happy to oblige. They arranged a date for early in the new year. Beverly closed her online calendar on her phone and popped her phone back in her bag. They all shook hands, wished each other "Merry Christmas" and Beverly turned to move to another group of guests, before the teenage girl blurted out to her turning back:

'Your pictures are a little bit like *Where's Wally*, aren't they?'

Beverly turned back to the young girl and looked surprised. 'I'm sorry?' she said. 'I don't understand.'

The teenage girl looked a little annoyed at having to explain. Trying not to, but letting her eyes roll, she said, 'Well you know. That man is in all the pictures, isn't he.'

Beverly had travelled extensively throughout her career, and her photographs in the exhibition today represented a span of over forty years. She really had no idea what the girl was talking about.

Beverly was about to let it go, but something nagged at her. Instead, Beverly said, 'I'm so sorry, I don't understand what you mean, but I look forward to seeing you all in January.' She smiled kindly at the young girl.

The teenage girl looked at her as though she was a little simple, and said, 'Let me show you.'

Beverly followed the teenage girl, champagne in hand and her eyebrows pulled together, puzzled.

The young girl took Beverly right to the start of

her career in the nineteen-eighties, when she was travelling around the West Coast of the USA. The photograph was taken in a bar, a jukebox lit with sounds in the corner, some people dancing, and in the opposite corner there was a man, sitting quietly, drinking a beer.

The girl pointed at him and said, 'That guy.'

Beverly looked at the man, puzzled. Then turned her puzzled look to the girl. So, the girl beckoned Beverly to follow her forward a decade. Beverly had been in London during the financial downturn of the nineteen-nineties. She'd taken some photographs in the North of England; mining had collapsed and real "salt of the earth" people were out and about in the damp town centres, grouping, talking, socialising. On a street corner, selling papers, was the same man again.

The teenage girl pointed at him and said, 'Look, it's the same guy.' Beverly leant forward and scrutinised the photograph. The teenage girl rolled her eyes and said, 'Right, follow me, five years later.' And walked along the wall to select the photograph she'd seen.

In the photo, there were crowds lining the Mall as the Queen and Nelson Mandela passed by in an ornate carriage, during his state visit to the UK. Beverly had been more interested in the crowds. In the shot of the adoring royalists, there was a policeman holding back the crowds, he was looking directly into Beverly's camera. The girl pointed and said, 'See, it's the same man.' Beverly looked at the photograph, opened-mouthed.

Once again, the teenage girl motioned Beverly forwards. Beverly was photographing people on a beach in Bali. Partygoers were seeing in the Millennium. People were dancing everywhere. Festoons of lights stretched from beach bar to beach bar. People were brandishing their multicoloured cocktails. The teenage girl pointed to a lone man sitting at the bar. He'd turned around and was looking directly into Beverly's camera. The girl said, 'See, here he is again.'

Beverly started to feel a little bit odd. She knew these photographs intimately. She'd scrutinised the negatives and smiled at the people she'd snapped. But she'd never noticed the same man was in all her photographs. It didn't make any sense. It must just be someone that looked similar each time.

Beverly turned to the teenage girl and said, 'Yes, I guess he does look like the same man, but it's probably just someone that looks very similar.'

The teenage girl managed to restrain herself from rolling her eyes at Beverly again, as she said, 'Oh, and by the way, he doesn't age in any of the photographs. Look for yourself. He's even in the photographs you took at Bestival in Dorset last summer.'

Beverly had no words. She just looked at the young girl open-mouthed.

The teenage girl's parents caught up with them. Along with their son, the parents thanked Beverly again for the wonderful exhibition, and politely shooed their children out.

Beverly turned back to the picture of the Queen's carriage and the policeman looking directly at her camera lens. Leaning forward she scrutinised the man's face. One of the exhibition guests tapped Beverly on the shoulder and said, 'I'd really like to know where you get your inspiration for the family portraits. I find them so natural and beautiful.'

Beverly straightened up, took a sip of champagne from her flute, tucked her bag firmly back under her arm again, and replied, 'Oh yes, absolutely. I. . .'

Beverly was troubled. How could a young girl see something so obvious, that she'd missed for over forty years of her life? The man was real. They were her photographs, she'd taken them, she'd developed them. She'd mounted them for tonight. The photographs and their occupants were real. Beverly could perhaps understand it if she'd had a lifelong partner, who had travelled with her while she was taking photographs, but Beverly had resolutely remained single all her life. It wasn't to say that she hadn't had her flings and her fun, but it was her work she was married to. Always. And she loved her work.

Beverly got home at nearly midnight on Christmas Eve. She couldn't help herself, she went straight to her studio and started searching through her photographs, looking for the man.

❄ ❄ ❄

Beverly barely managed to eat her Christmas dinner, and she only just managed to return the phone calls that she absolutely had to; family and very close friends. She was obsessed with finding the man. In total, he was in fifty-two pictures, spanning forty-three years. And he never seemed to age. It was absolutely bizarre.

Beverly sat down heavily on her mustard-coloured velvet sofa in front of a late-night Christmas film. She was completely bemused and at a loss to explain how this was happening. The film started and she could feel her eyes feeling weary. She was probably overtired; she'd been working too hard. It must all be a mistake, an illusion. She'd looked at too many photographs today, and in preparing for the exhibition, she just needed to get some to sleep.

* * *

In her dreams, Beverly was doing what she loved to do. She had her camera around her neck and from behind the lens she was viewing the world. A world slightly different to how other people saw it, instead it was how she saw it. How she wanted others to see it. Directing people to focus on subjects that she wanted them to think about: love, family, memories, injustices, tradition, romance.

In her dream, Beverly found herself at the entrance to a church. She was the wedding photographer and she was late. She remembered feeling panicked and checking that she had all her equipment with her as she rushed into the church. At the front of the church, in front of the altar, stood the bride and groom. The priest was before them, just about to pronounce them man and wife, just as Beverly had burst into the church. The bride and groom turned around. To Beverly's shock, she saw that the bride was her and the groom was the man in the photographs.

* * *

Beverly was troubled like she'd never been before. She'd looked at too many photographs. She'd been having strange dreams. She needed to give it a break. Maybe she was overworked? Beverly decided to spend a few days with her brother and get away from the photographs.

Packing a small suitcase into her car, alongside her beloved camera equipment, Beverly locked up her apartment, and travelled the few hundred miles to her brother's house. If it was comfortable with them, perhaps she'd stay until New Year. She needed a break. She'd been overworking, that was all.

Beverly's brother and his wife were delighted to host her, but word got around that Beverly was staying for a rare visit, and soon the extended family piled around too. All her nieces and nephews and their children. Beverly naturally fell into the role of observer behind the lens. She took photographs of her family and delighted them all with the forever memories she recorded. Beverly was always the one behind the camera, and never in the photo. There were actually very few photographs of her, because she'd spent most of her life watching, studying and looking at other people.

Beverly, her brother, and his wife decided they'd all collectively eaten too much and should walk it off in the park. While they were walking her brother suggested that he should take a photograph of her.

Acquiescing, Beverly sat down by a fountain and looked up, as he fiddled with the knobs on her camera, and moved the lens in and out.

Snap, snap, snap.

He came over to her, so that she could check the photographs through the viewfinder, and she said, 'You know, you really are very good. A natural photographer.' Her brother scoffed at the praise, but he was flattered, nonetheless.

Beverly stayed until the New Year and she spent a very pleasant New Year's Eve with her brother and sister-in-law. But, by the time New Year's Day came around, she found herself itching to get back to her work. Besides, she still had the orders to mop up from her Christmas Eve exhibition.

Driving back home and ascending the lift, she entered the quiet calm of her apartment, and within an hour, she was getting to work on developing her family Christmas photographs.

It was strange seeing a photograph of herself.

Beverly very rarely had her photo taken, and she wasn't part of the selfie generation (narcissism wasn't her vibe). She took out her loupe and inspected the photograph of her by the fountain. To her shock, she found in the background, walking a dog, was the man.

Beverly looked again. Definitely and absolutely the same man. He had short brown hair; a round face with quite a pointed nose; and wide-set, sparkling, blue eyes. He was clean-shaven and looked perhaps thirty-five or forty years old. His stance was relaxed and as in all the photographs, and he always wore a leather jacket (except for the photograph when he was the policeman). Forty-three years had passed, how could he look the same?

Beverly felt a little bit shaky. She decided to stop work for tonight and make herself some dinner.

❋ ❋ ❋

The next morning, Beverly got to work fulfilling the Christmas Eve orders, and reviewing her appointments for the next two weeks. When lunchtime came around, she decided to give herself a little break. One of her favourite things to do was to go down to the park, walk around, and take photographs. Photographs of happy couples talking as if there was no one else in the world; children playing on the climbing frames; old people still in love and holding hands. All the things that made Beverly happy.

With her beloved camera around her neck, Beverly waited for just the right moment to capture people looking relaxed and happy. Nowadays, she always made sure that she asked permission and if they didn't want their photographs in an exhibition, then she deleted them. Beverly easily spent an hour taking photographs of loved-up couples wrapped up against the cold; small children trying out their new Christmas bikes and tricycles; and dog owners doing their twice-daily walks.

Finding the café in the park, Beverly ordered herself the cranberry and brie panini and a hot cappuccino to drink. She sat huddled up on one of the metal frame chairs outside the café. She watched people pass by as she ate. It was something she loved to do.

Absentmindedly, Beverly raised the camera to her eye and scanned around a few scenes in front of her. Shocked, she saw in the middle distance, a man sat on the bench and it looked like *the* man.

Beverly removed the camera from her eye, and blinking in the winter sunshine, she looked again. But there was nobody there. Shakily she raised the camera to her face again and looked through the viewfinder. There he was! But this time he raised his arm and waved at her. Beverly hastily dropped the camera back onto her lap and tried to not think about it, as she finished eating her panini.

When she had finished her lunch, Beverly drained the last of her cappuccino, and tried to relax back into the hard metal chair. She was starting to feel chilly, and she needed to get back to work. However, curiosity over the man on the bench got the better of her, and she couldn't help herself, as she picked up the camera, and looked again at the bench in the middle distance through the viewfinder. He was still there, but he was looking away from her, watching some children on the metal climbing frames.

Suddenly, Beverly decided that life was too short, and she needed to find out what this was all about. So, clutching her camera tightly, she started to walk towards the bench.

❊ ❊ ❊

Beverly remembered that the man had been sitting on the right-hand side of the bench. The bench was completely empty when she approached, and she carefully sat on the left-hand side of the bench. She tried to appear relaxed as she slowly lifted her camera to her eye and looked through the viewfinder. Beverly scanned around to her left, to see if anyone was sitting with her.

There he was. No more than a few feet from her, looking straight at her, and smiling and waving. If he was a ghost, he didn't seem very scary. In fact, he felt familiar, as if she'd known him all her life. In a strange way she guessed she had known him all her life, as he'd always been in her photographs, it was just that *she'd* never noticed him before.

Beverly found her hands were shaking, as she continued to hold the camera to her face and (knowing she probably sounded like a lunatic to any stranger passing by) she asked with a tremble in her voice, 'Who are you?'

Beverly could see his lips moving but she couldn't hear any words. She shook her head and she said, 'I can't hear you.'

The man stopped talking and instead, he tried to sign to her. He made several gestures with his hands. It was quite expressive and confusing, but one gesture caught her attention quite clearly; when he put his left hand over his heart and covered it by his right hand, and smiled.

Beverly tried again. She asked, 'Why have you been in my photographs and waiting for me here?'

The man smiled and shrugged and then pointed to the watch on his wrist and smiled and shrugged again.

Beverly didn't really know what to do, and she wasn't sure what to make of all of this, so she said, 'Don't follow me home. I don't want you to come to my home, but I'll take a photograph of you now if that's okay?'

The man nodded vigorously, "Yes." and tried to pose, his face fully facing her camera lens.

Snap, snap, snap.

'Thank you.' Beverly said.

The air outside was cool, and the people that had come out for their lunch were starting to disperse. Beverly didn't really know what to make of all of this. She was curious, but she was a little bit worried too. She looked over at the empty bench, and to thin air said, 'I'll develop the photographs, and perhaps I'll see you again tomorrow.'

The man nodded vigorously, "Yes." and waved goodbye to her.

* * *

Beverly found it difficult to concentrate on her work. She couldn't help herself, she had to develop the photographs from the park today. She went into her developing room, to enlarge and develop the photographs. Beverly hung them to dry. He was there in the images but she didn't stop to think, she just went mechanically about her work.

While waiting for the photographs to dry, Beverly tried to busy herself with her day-to-day work about the apartment. Later in the afternoon she came back to her washing line of surprises, taking the photographs off the line, she used her loupe to inspect the images. He was sat on the bench smiling at her, his kind eyes looking directly at her, waving. He seemed familiar. Beverly shook her head, was she going mad? If she was getting dementia, she should book an appointment with the doctor.

Ringing the doctor's surgery, they gave her an urgent appointment for six weeks' time. Thanking them, Beverly hung up the call and called some friends and family to install a little bit of normality into her life. Not that she was going to talk about this incident at all. People really would think she'd lost it.

※ ※ ※

The next morning, Beverly popped the photographs of him into a large brown envelope and thoughtfully she also picked up a notepad and a pen. At lunchtime she went back to the park again, but she wasn't interested in the comings and goings of the everyday people, she was looking for him.

Repeatedly, Beverly lifted her camera and scanned around for him, particularly checking the benches. Within ten minutes she'd found him and she walked over, sitting down just like she had the day before.

Beverly took out the photographs from the brown paper envelope, and checking that nobody was within earshot, she said, 'I have these photographs of you from yesterday, so I know you must be real.' Then she added, 'I also brought a pad and a pen, because I can't hear you, but I'm hoping that you might be able to write something to me.'

Beverly's hand shook a little as she pushed the pad and pen across the bench to where she knew he had been sitting. She sat back against the bench, but the pad and the pen didn't move. So, she tried a different tactic, and lifted the camera to her face, looking through the viewfinder. In it, she saw that he'd picked up the pad and he quickly wrote: *Ask me any question.*

Removing the camera from her face, Beverly looked down and saw the pad untouched on the bench. She pulled her eyebrows together, puzzled, and looked back again through the viewfinder of her camera. She asked her first question to the air, 'Who are you?'

Through the viewfinder, Beverly saw the man smile and he wrote on the pad, turning it around so that she could see his answer. It read: *I'm your soul mate.*

Beverly would have laughed, if it wasn't so concerning. She did not believe in soulmates. She was married to her work. Beverly asked another question, 'If you are my soul mate, then why aren't we together?'

Again, he smiled and picked up the pad. He scribbled a reply, turning the pad around he'd written: *Because you're so busy with your work. I don't want to disturb you. You're happy.*

Beverly asked another question, 'Why are you in so many of my photographs? Why are you hanging around?'

The man smiled again, and picking up the pad he wrote a long reply: *Because I'm waiting for you to be finished being single, so that we can be together. You don't have time in your life for me right now, and that's okay, I'm happy to wait. I've waited forty-three years, I can wait a few more.*

'Did I meet you forty-three years ago?' Beverly

asked.

The man wrote furiously, then turned the pad so she could see his answer: *No, we've been married before, several times, in our other lives. So, you see, we have all the time in the world.*

Beverly asked, 'Is something about to happen to me? Is this why I can see you now?'

The man shook his head vigorously, "No" and put his hand to his heart, and he wrote: *Not at all. You've just never noticed me before.*

Beverly removed the camera from her face and retrieving the pad and pen she said to the air, 'I need to think about this. Maybe I'll come back tomorrow.'

❊ ❊ ❊

Beverly didn't go back to the park the next day. She needed some time to think about this. She wasn't afraid of the man, but this was all quite strange. She'd had lovers and relationships before, but nothing seemed to stick. She'd always been married to her work and loved her job. Was there really anything more to discover? Had she been missing out on some other dimension of life? And how was she going to interact with someone that she could only see through the lens of her camera? It didn't make any sense at all.

Beverly tried to focus on her work in the day, and at night get some rest and count down the days until she had her dementia checks. One thing she did do, was to take one of the photographs of the man in the park and put it in a picture frame on the coffee table. She needed a reality check that this really did happen. And she needed to think about it.

It wasn't something that she normally did, but Beverly was starting to wonder if she'd missed out on something in life. She thought about all the people who were partnered up, like Marie and Jeremy, her brother and sister-in-law, and the family at the gallery exhibition. Beverly had always been so busy with her work, that she'd never considered it before. What did they do with their time? Why would you want to be around someone all the time? It seemed so alien to her.

Beverly was curious about the dynamics of romantic relationships, so she went on to Netflix and decided to watch some romcoms (completely unlike her). She worked her way through many classics. You'd have to have a cold heart not to cry at the film *Ghost*. Beverly was struck by the thought, is this what was happening to her? Some previous-life husband come back to watch her?

Beverly must have fallen asleep on the sofa, because the next thing she remembered was hearing a man's voice saying to her, 'Beverly, Beverly? Are you awake?'

Beverly was so tired, that she didn't want to open her eyes. Peeking out she could see that she was in her living room, her head was resting on a cushion, before her was the picture of the man she'd placed on her coffee table. The man in the photograph was waving manically and beckoning her to come with him – into the picture. Beverly held out her hand, and strangely, he reached out his hand towards her.

Suddenly, Beverly found herself in the photograph. All around her, she was surrounded by the park, but it wasn't the photograph, it was the park exactly as it was on the day that she'd taken the photograph, except he was standing before her as if he'd always been.

'What's your name?' Beverly asked.

'Richard.' The man simply replied, in his deep resonating voice.

'Why do you follow me?'

'Because I love you, and I can't bear to be without you. I love seeing you happy, taking your photographs. It gives me joy.'

'But I don't know anything about you.'

Richard thoughtfully wiped his hand over his mouth and said, 'Yes. That's true. I know a lot about you.' Richard suddenly looked like he'd had a good idea, excitedly he suggested, 'Why don't we go on a date?'

Beverly would have laughed, but she realised that he was completely serious. Incredulously she said, 'But I'm at least thirty years older than you.'

Richard raised his eyebrows, 'That doesn't make mathematical sense. I've been in forty-three years' worth of photographs.'

Beverly tried to do the maths in her head. Shaking her head, she asked, 'So how old are you?'

Richard respectfully replied, 'I'm outside of time. It's irrelevant. Do you pick your dates on what car they drive?'

'No.'

'So, if age is a non-issue,' and in so saying his eyes softened, 'I would be honoured if you would let me take you on a date.'

Beverly had exhausted all of her logical questions. She had no more arguments left, so she respectfully replied, 'Okay then. Thank you, Richard. Let's go on a date so I can learn a little more about you.'

* * *

Beverly awoke in the bright winter sunshine, achy from sleeping on the sofa all night. She'd had the strangest dream where she'd met Richard, the man in the photograph.

Beverly looked at the photograph sitting on her coffee table. She had a strange feeling. It was the first time she'd ever felt something like this. The apartment felt empty, and Beverly felt as though she was missing something.

Shaking her head, Beverly went through her morning routine. The day was busy and she didn't really get much time to think about Richard. When it came to the evening, she decided to watch another romcom. but she didn't want to be there with the photograph of Richard anymore, so she put him in her bedroom.

The film was very sweet, it was lovely to see two people so devoted to each other, but it was so abstract from her reality that she found it hard to relate to. The men in her life had never acted like that, they'd never really taken care of her, or shown her much interest, and most didn't even listen to her. It was more about having a plus one for events, or dinner dates, or other physical things. But the films showed people caring for each other, craving each other, and wanting to be around the other person as much as possible. Cognitively, Beverly knew relationships like that existed, but it wasn't her reality.

That night Beverly fell into a restless sleep, and once again she woke to her name being called:

'Beverly, Beverly, come with me.'

Beverly opened her eyes, and in her dream again, Richard was waving at her from the photograph, beckoning her to come with him.

Beverly got out of bed and walked over to the picture. Stretching out her hand, Richard reached forward to pull her into the picture with him.

Richard was delighted to see her again. He asked her how her day had been, and listened to her reply. He then asked if she wanted to get some lunch with him? Beverly agreed, and they walked over to the little café in the park, chatting about this and that, laughing at some silly jokes or talking about her photography.

Beverly felt good being around Richard, she felt

like he was actually listening to what she was saying, as if he was interested in her. The more they talked, the more Beverly started to understand him, she found that she was becoming increasingly sensitive to small changes in the pitch of his voice, or the words he used, or interpreting the emotions that passed over his face. It was almost as if she was learning to read him.

* * *

Beverly found she was dreaming more and more about meeting Richard in the park. In reality, she wasn't going back to the park at lunchtimes at all. But in her dreams, she was there every night with him, and the more she was around him, the more she liked him and wanted to be around him. The more she discovered Richard, the more Beverly found her waking days lonelier and emptier than before.

Until one night.

Beverly was with Richard in her dream. He had walked her to the fountain, got down on one knee, and asked her to marry him.

Beverly clasped her hand over her mouth, and little tears sprang to her eyes. Without thinking she said, 'Yes.' Because she couldn't think of anyone in the world that she would rather be with than Richard.

Richard was delighted. Getting up, and holding hands with Beverly, he pulled her gently towards him and kissed her lightly on the mouth. His lips were soft and he smelt of fresh pine cones, and security and safety. Beverly buried her face into his chest and wrapped her arms around his torso inside his coat. Richard lightly kissed the top of her head, saying, 'You don't know how much I've missed holding you. You don't know how long I've waited for you.' And he buried his head in her hair.

Beverly replied, in a muffled voice from his chest, 'Forty-three years.'

Richard laughed through his tears. He said, 'Yes, just to have this moment with you. I must be crazy, or in love. Quite possibly both.' He tried to suck in his breath, to be a man and not cry. To distract himself he suggested they do something practical. Excitedly he said to Beverly, 'We should go and buy a ring! I don't want anyone to whisk you away. I want the world to know you are mine.'

They sauntered along the pavement, hand in hand, and looked in jeweller's windows, but nothing seemed quite right, until they came to an antique jewellery shop. In the window was a large, three-carat emerald, square cut, surrounded by smaller diamonds.

Immediately, Beverly said, 'That one.' and pointed, 'That's the one.'

Richard smiled down at her saying, 'Let's go in.' and holding her hand, he led her in through the jeweller's door.

* * *

Beverly's brother stood dazed holding the telephone as he tried to take in what Marie was telling him. On the kitchen table in front of him sat a brown envelope, inside were the family photographs Beverly had taken over Christmas. She'd sent them a week ago. He asked, 'What's happened?'

Marie's voice cracked a little as she re-explained down the line. 'She was supposed to go to a dementia appointment, and the surgery couldn't get hold of her, and she had me down as next of kin, because I think you're quite far away. I couldn't get hold of her either, and Jeremy tried too. I was beside myself with worry. We decided to get the police to break into her apartment. I'm so sorry to tell you this, but it looks like she's passed away in her sleep. We are just waiting for the death certificate.'

Beverly's brother held his hand over his eyes as big fat tears spontaneously rolled out. He said, 'Oh my goodness.' and tried to argue, 'But she was in perfect health, what could have happened?'

Marie replied, 'We don't know, but it looks like there was a man involved.'

'Really?' His sister was married to her work, she showed little interest in men. Ever.

'Yes.' Marie replied, 'When they found her in bed, she was wearing an engagement ring and a wedding ring but they couldn't find signs of anyone else in the apartment.'

Beverly's brother shook his head, as his mind reeled with the information, 'But she didn't tell me she was seeing anybody.'

'She didn't tell me anything either. It's just not like her. But if she did get married it looks like it was recent. They said they're going to check with the registrar. Of course, this could affect your inheritance. . .'

Beverly's brother was lost for words. His sister, who for the whole of her life had been married to her work, suddenly found love and got married weeks before she passed away? Something didn't seem right. He knew his sister. She wasn't the type to die for love.

9.   THE PRIEST AND THE PROSTITUTE

Father Columba was buffeted by the cold winds coming in from the sea, which pushed him against the rough hillside. His red-chapped hands held the fork, while his mud-encrusted boots, encasing cold weary feet, pushed at the fork to dig up the winter potatoes from the hillside garden. Father Columba was a tall man with long features. His hair had started turning grey and he kept his beard long. Easing his aching back and standing for a moment, Father Columba turned around to look at the views around him, on the island of Iona.

The island stood proud, a stone testament of nature, topped by a man-made stone temple; the Abbey of Iona giving its glory to God. Father Columba was lucky to live here and he knew it. In front of him, Father Columba could see further downhill to the stone structure of the Abbey sat amidst green manicured grass and surrounded by Celtic crosses and little pathways. The Abbey looked out from the green and brown scrubby island, onto the cool-blue and grey waters that surrounded them. As his eyes wandered beyond the waters, other grey, rocky crags emerged from the cool, salty waves, almost as if they were giant stepping stones, making paths over the water. Father Columba sighed deeply; he was so lucky to be here; God's heaven on earth.

Reaching down his red-chapped hands, Father Columba pulled out the last few potatoes to fill the sack. Holding the sack tightly in one hand and the rusty fork in the other, he joined with two more of his fellow brethren, as they walked back to the Abbey, and discussed excitedly what meat they would be having for their Christmas dinner. Although they were humble and rationed the food they ate, Christmas was always a celebration. They allowed themselves to think of the delicious food and how it would fill their stomachs. Father Columba was so excited. He loved this time of year; he was so lucky to be here.

✽ ✽ ✽

Father Columba placed the sack of potatoes down in the Abbey kitchen, next to the two other sacks his fellow brethren had dug up, just as Father Michael rushed in to find him.

Father Michael touched Father Columba on the shoulder and said, 'Your brother is in the main hall. He has come over from the mainland to see you.'

Hastily washing his red-chapped hands in hot soapy water, and making them even redder, Father Columba rushed as quickly as he could to see his younger brother. Next to God, Ray was the person he loved most in the world.

Upon entering the hall, the brothers' eyes connected in the close bond that they had shared since childhood.

Ray looked like his brother in every way, except he his hair was brown and he kept it short. Although Father Columba's brother had not entered the priesthood, he did believe in God and they had talked deeply on many matters, including religion, philosophy and even girls. It made Father Columba sad that his brother had not found his calling; he'd not yet found what he was supposed to do in life. Just like the little boats that Father Columba watched in the bay, his younger brother seemed to be tormented by the storms that passed through his life. Father Columba wished he could do more to help, but he couldn't live his brother's life for him, all he could do was hold his hand along the path he chose to walk.

Father Columba bear-hugged his brother and held onto him tightly, his eyes welled with joy.

'Ray! I'm so glad to see you. How are you?' Father Columba held his younger brother back a little bit and looked sensitively into his eyes.

His brother shook his head sadly and looked down at the floor. 'Well, you know, the usual ups and downs.' Ray looked up to his brother's caring eyes. 'I feel good seeing you, and having some time to talk with you. Perhaps I'll be able to make it out again before Christmas?'

Father Columba said, 'I would be delighted. I'm sorry I can't give you as much time as I used to, but you're always in my prayers, always.' The brothers hugged each other again, secure in their fraternal love.

Father Columba was so glad to see Ray. Already this was going to be one of the best Christmases ever. Comfortably they took seats at the end of one of the long tables nearest the fire in the main hall, and talked for an hour or more. Father Columba's friend, Father Michael brought them some warm, sweet tea, and some honey and oat biscuits made at the Abbey. They were delicious.

❋ ❋ ❋

Father Michael rushed to collect Father Columba from his position by the sink, where he was scrubbing the mud off the cold, hard potatoes. Gasping at his breath, Father Michael said, 'The Abbot wants to see you.'

Father Columba looked up from his task, and smiled, 'Is he in his office? I'll be along soon.'

Father Michael shook his head urgently, 'No, he said you must come now.'

Father Columba raised his eyebrows in surprise, and quickly drying his hands he chucked off his apron and followed Father Michael. They passed out of the kitchen, along the side of the stone-carved quad, which enclosed a green square of manicured grass, and into another part of the building, where the Abbot resided in his warm office.

Feeling he had done his duty, Father Michael left his friend at the door, with a reassuring squeeze on his shoulder.

Father Columba sat uncomfortably waiting to be summoned.

Finally, the Abbot called to him, 'Come in.' from behind the door.

Father Columba reached for the old, wrought-iron, solid, black, door handle; in the three-inch-thick, dark-brown, old, oak wooden door, and heavily pushed it backwards to allow him entry into the room.

The Abbot had his desk by the window, so that he could look out onto the sea. He was stood by the window as Father Columba came into the room, and he motioned Father Columba over to the fire.

They took a chair each as the Abbot said to him, 'Dear Father Columba, you are such an asset to this Abbey. You are aware we are all here to do God's work.'

Father Columba nodded and said, 'It is my calling. Every day I wish to be a blessing in everything that I do. I feel lucky that this is my path.'

The Abbot smiled tightly and said, 'Yes, I know that is how you feel and that is why I knew that you would jump at the opportunity to do God's work in Bolton.'

'Bolton!' Father Columba tried not to sound surprised.

'Yes, Bolton.' the Abbot confirmed. Slowly and in a measured tone he continued, 'They have need for someone with your particular skills and there are many souls to be saved. You have done good work at the Abbey here, and you have led a prayerful life, but God is calling you to do other work, and we must all answer God's call willingly.'

Father Columba did care about God, really, he did. But selfishly, in the moment, all he could think about was the beautiful island and wild seas of Iona, the turkey and goose that they would be having for Christmas lunch, and the visits from his brother who lived on the mainland. Father Columba's heart sank as he nodded in acquiescence to his abbot.

✽ ✽ ✽

Father Columba joined Father Friend in the presbytery. It was seven p.m. on a dark and drizzly Saturday night, two weeks before Christmas. They'd had a dinner of spaghetti hoops on toast. Looking out the window, Father Columba noted the damp seemed to permeate every inch of the air and vegetation outside. Father Columba looked warily at Father Friend, as he busied around the presbytery, grabbing his coat and scarf, and a thermos of tea to put in his rucksack, to keep them going. Father Friend was a short stocky man with sharp features, wild grey hair, and quick mannerisms.

Father Columba pulled his coat a little tighter

around him. He wondered, "What was the worst that could happen?" He knew he was here to do God's work but going out on the dangerous streets of Bolton, late on a Saturday night to save souls, wasn't exactly what he'd imagined when he'd answered God's calling.

Father Friend turned to his new houseguest, and smiling in an easy way, he asked, 'Ready?'

Resigned to his fate, Father Columba just replied, 'Yes.' and nodded his head sadly. He'd always quite liked his nose the way it was. He didn't want to get into any fights and have a broken nose.

They carefully exited the presbytery, locked the door (the presbytery had been burgled three times in the last five years) shuffled along the slippery, damp paths in the suburbs, and turned their feet towards the rough part of town.

As they walked along the pavement, Father Columba winced every time he heard a car go racing by, and he cringed inside when he heard the loud, beatbox music. It was in these moments that he longed for the peace of Iona. But courageously he put his trust back in God and soldiered bravely on.

Father Friend found a homeless man sleeping in an old shop entrance. He was wrapped in a sleeping bag and surrounded by cardboard to try and keep out the winter winds. His beard had grown so wild that it filled the crevices of his face. Most of his teeth were missing, but despite his slurred speech and disjointed movements, the man's eyes were kind, sad and despondent, but kind. The two priests prayed with the man for a short while, and Father Friend tried to encourage the man to go to one of the shelters, or at the very least go to the soup kitchen. But they couldn't force him out of his little cardboard snug, and so eventually they moved on.

On the street corner, there stood a lady with dark-red dyed hair, wearing a faux fur coat and high, stiletto heels. She looked as though she was dressed for a night on the town. Quietly, Father Friend said to Father Columba, 'Here we have a chance to save some souls.' He removed his hand from his mouth and turned to the lady, smiled and walked towards her, with Father Columba in tow.

Father Friend said, 'How are you? Do you feel comfortable to say a prayer with us?'

The lady looked the priests up and down, and as if she'd been punched in the heart, she sighed a deep sigh. 'Yes Father, I would be glad to say a prayer with you, but would you pray for my protection tonight?'

Father Friend nodded, and with a small tear at the corner of his eye, he said, 'It would be an honour.' He took a deep breath, made the sign of the cross, followed by Father Columba and the lady, and started, 'Saint Michael the Archangel, defend us in battle, be our protection. . .' The winter wind fell from a rush to whisper, and a gentle calm fell upon the group of three. The priest finished his prayers and they wished each other "God bless" as the two priests moved on.

Father Columba was beginning to realise that rather than feeling afraid for himself and his own physical body, he truly was at the frontline of the battleground for saving souls. He had a job to do, and he could carry on in the shadows and feel worried for himself, or he could bravely step forward and peacefully make his voice count.

The two priests rounded a corner where several girls frequented the street. Father Friend quietly suggested to Father Columba that they each take a side and pray with the ladies. With a pat on the back from Father Friend, Father Columba walked bravely forward and politely introduced himself to the group of ladies.

Two of the prostitutes looked him up and down, and one swore at him saying, 'Last time I prayed with one of you, I didn't get any business for a week. It's nearly Christmas, and I've got a child to buy presents for and put food in his mouth. Not tonight, Father, I don't want your prayers.' Linking arms with another lady, they walked away. But one lady stayed, she was very young and she looked a little scared.

Father Columba gently turned to her and asked, 'And you, Miss? Will you say a simple prayer to the Lord with me, so that he may keep you safe tonight?'

Shakily, the young lady nodded, her head of chestnut-coloured ringlets swishing gently around her young, pale skin, which was covered by her bright makeup art. She seemed so young.

Together, the priest and the prostitute joined in prayer as they made the sign of the cross.

✳ ✳ ✳

Father Friend thought it was a delightful idea that Father Columba invite his younger brother to stay with them over Christmas. The two priests had had conversations late into the night, and Father Friend was very aware that Father Columba worried about his younger brother, Ray. Ray was an introvert who hadn't found his way in life. Father Friend was ever eager to be open and warm to those who were walking around in the half-light, not knowing quite what they should do. Father Friend thought that they might have some very interesting theological discussions, which may form Ray's opinion one way or the other.

Father Columba was delighted to receive his brother a few days before Christmas. They embraced warmly when Ray had alighted from the train, at the station in Bolton. It had been a long journey, but Ray had been glad to do it, and at the very least they got to spend Christmas together.

Ray got into the Christmas spirit. He attended most of the Christmas sermons with Father Columba and helped out at the coffee mornings. He even attended one of Father Friend's evening prayer sessions.

✳ ✳ ✳

It was Christmas Eve and the winter weather had turned particularly cold. Midnight Mass was scheduled for early evening, for the sake of the children. After Mass, the three men sat down in the presbytery dining room, for an evening meal of stew. Father Columba explained to Ray that Father Friend had encouraged him out, late at night, onto the streets of Bolton, to pray with the people and help save souls.

Ray was very interested and said, 'Well Christmas isn't just about the presents, is it? It is about the baby Jesus coming to earth to save souls.'

Both the priests chuckled and Father Friend said, 'I couldn't have said it better myself.'

Ray smiled and turned to his brother, 'So how did it go? What did you do?'

Father Columba replied, 'The most important thing is to pray with the people you meet. Sometimes the homeless, or the drug addicts, or the prostitutes. I was scared at first, but the worst I've had is to be sworn at. Most people are kind.'

Ray exclaimed, 'Prostitutes!'

'Why, yes.' Father Columba replied, 'Every human soul deserves God's love and protection.'

At that moment a particularly gusty blast of wind rattled the Victorian sheet pane windows in the presbytery, and all three men looked out onto the cold, gloomy night.

Ray said, 'Do you think the homeless are out there tonight?'

Father Friend shook his head sadly and replied,

'Yes. Unfortunately, yes.'

Ray exclaimed, 'But this doesn't feel right. You have all these community buildings, surely tonight there is something you can do to get them out of the cold?'

Father Friend shook his head sadly, 'We've tried opening the church before, or leaving it open over Christmas, but unfortunately people come in and steal the candlesticks. So, after Mass, we lock up the church until the Christmas morning service.'

Ray looked at his brother and said, 'This just doesn't feel right. We can't leave the homeless out on a cold night like tonight, not when Jesus came into the world, and that's what we're celebrating. Is there not something else we could do?'

Father Columba shrugged sadly at his brother and shook his head, but Father Friend mused a little. He rubbed his fingers along his lips and said, 'I guess we could offer shelter in the parish hall, just for tonight. I have spare biscuits, tea and coffee in the storeroom. I have spare blankets that we use to cover the tables for this summer's fête. I guess for tonight I won't get into too much trouble, if we give them somewhere warm.'

All three men smiled at each other. They had a plan.

∗ ∗ ∗

While Father Friend cheered up the parish hall, dragged out the blankets, and started making some teas and coffees, Father Columba and his brother went back out to the streets of Bolton, in the cold and the dark, to offer somewhere warm for tonight to the poor homeless that couldn't make it to the shelters.

Father Columba had a much better time with the man with the sad eyes and the big beard under his cardboard box, and he managed to persuade him to go to the safety of the parish hall and get a biscuit and a cup of tea. The brothers managed to find another five people, and encourage them back to the parish hall, before they came to a lumpy sleeping bag, huddled in a corner, beside a shop, in an alleyway not far from where Father Columba had seen Father Friend pray for the first time with a prostitute.

Ray knelt gently next to the bundle and said to the cold shivering human, 'Will you come with us? We have some shelter for you tonight at the church parish hall, there are blankets and tea and coffee. Will you come out of the cold?'

Two brown eyes peeked out from over the sleeping bag, and some greasy, chestnut-coloured ringlets stuck to the side of the young girl's face, as she took in the two men before her. She drew her eyebrows together in anger and pointed at Father Columba saying, 'You! It is your fault that I have lost everything. It is you. You prayed a prayer on me and no man would go near me. I couldn't get any money. I couldn't pay the rent. I'm homeless because of you.'

Ray took a sharp intake of breath, as did Father Columba. Father Columba stood there, shivering in the cold and the dark, looking down sadly at the prostitute that he'd prayed to Michael to protect, and feeling terrible that his actions had led her to lose her home and end up on the streets. He felt personally responsible.

Ray turned to his brother with inquiring eyes, and Father Columba returned his brother's look with a little sad shrug under an upside-down mouth. He watched as his younger brother, Ray, tend to the vulnerable woman, and gently persuade her to come with them, to find shelter in the church parish hall tonight.

※ ※ ※

Father Columba and his brother Ray did well. They managed to find twelve people in total to bring in out of the cold. These poor people were covered with extra blankets and given a warm drink and a sweet biscuit. Father Friend had done a wonderful job preparing the white china cups and saucers, heating the hot water urn and arranging the biscuits better than any of the ladies from afternoon coffee.

Ray and Father Columba went from person to person, checking on their personal state and saying little prayers with them. When it came to the prostitute with the chestnut-brown ringlet hair, Ray seemed particularly sensitive to her needs, and knelt beside her as both men prayed with her. Father Columba could feel that Ray felt very sorry for this poor woman. Her name was Ellen.

When they had finished doing their prayer rounds. Ray specifically went to talk to Ellen. Father Columba looked over protectively at his younger brother. He couldn't help but feel surprised, knowing how awkward Ray was around women.

In the hush of the hall, little phrases drifted over to Father Columba '. . .Harry Potter. . . Moomins. . . Pokémon. . .' Father Columba was confused, were they discussing children's cartoons and toys? He busied himself with the biscuits and tried not to look.

Father Columba and Ray returned to Father Friend, who explained the guests that they would be safe here tonight, and leaving them with a small lamp on in the corner, the three men returned to the presbytery to get a little sleep before the early morning Mass.

❋ ❋ ❋

The next morning the two priests and Ray went to check on their guests. Some had already left and some were in the process of packing up, before the parishioners arrived for the Christmas Day Mass. One or two were going to try and find a soup kitchen to get a little something to eat, and Father Friend assured them that if they wished to come back tonight, then he would again open up the hall for one more night (knowing that he was going to get told off by the bishop).

Ray took particular care to make sure that Ellen had packed up all her things, and Father Columba noticed him slip her a little money to get something to eat today. Father Columba wished he hadn't done that, because it looked like he was giving preferential treatment to Ellen, and there was a high likelihood that she might spend it on drugs. But he couldn't control his brother, so he just watched on, warily.

✣ ✣ ✣

The three men had a very pleasant Christmas Day together. Ray attended Mass with Father Columba and Father Friend, as they worked their way through the Christmas services. Ray met with the parishioners for mince pies and coffees and watched the priests in their pastoral roles. Then they all had a very enjoyable roast for a late lunch.

After lunch, Father Friend opened a bottle of scotch that a kind parishioner had given to him at Christmas, and they all enjoyed a dram.

That evening, Father Columba and Father Friend collected the spare mince pies and made ready to open the parish hall again. A few of the homeless guests from the previous night had already gathered outside. Father Friend had made it clear last night that they were welcome to come back tonight too, but of course, not all of them would come.

Ray looked around hopefully for Ellen, but she hadn't arrived yet. Father Columba tried to busy himself with filling the teapot from the hot water urn. Outside a cold rain started to patter on the windows and roof. Again, Ray looked outside worriedly. Father Columba knew he was looking for Ellen.

After an agonising wait of at least another half an hour, Ellen finally stumbled through the door of the parish hall, cold and wet from the rain. She gratefully accepted a blanket, mince pie and a warm cup of coffee. She sat down at one of the tables and Ray immediately went to join her. Father Columba could see them talking, and Ray shaking his head at what she told him.

Father Friend and Father Columba went around to visit their guests and took time to pray with each of them. When they came to Ellen, Ray was still with her.

Ray explained, 'Poor Ellen has had a little difficulty with some of the other "ladies". They don't understand why she's "making things difficult for herself and not trying a bit harder" to get business. One of them has offered her a place to get her back into the game, but I'm trying to persuade Ellen not to do it.'

Father Columba came to his brother's aid and said gently to Ellen, 'I am positive that God has a very special job for you, but you will be tempted to do other things along that road. All I can tell you is when he reveals his job to you, you won't be hesitating, because you'll know in your heart it is the right thing for you. You will have a burning desire to do it. It will be something you feel strongly about. It won't feel like a chore to get up in the morning, it will feel like a purpose, and it will be something you are uniquely made to do. Small skills and talents that you didn't know were useful, will become useful. God doesn't make mistakes. He has designed you for a specific purpose. If you give yourself to him, he will open the pathways for you. I promise.'

Ray and Ellen looked at Father Columba and Father Friend hopefully. All four of them put their hands together to pray.

* * *

Later that evening, when the priests and Ray had left their guests to cosy up for the night, the men chatted quietly in the warm sitting room at the presbytery. Father Columba could tell that there was something on Ray's mind, and he thought he knew what it was.

Father Columba could see that Ray's heart was opening to the young lady, Ellen, and as a protective older brother, he didn't know how he felt about that. He wanted his brother to find a companion in life, but he wasn't sure that this young lady was the right companion and influence for Ray.

It wasn't until they turned in for the night that Father Columba got his answer. While Father Friend went around the presbytery, checking everything was locked and turned off, Ray took the opportunity to talk quietly to his brother.

Ray said, 'I feel it. Just like you said when you know the right path, you'll feel and you'll know it's the right path because you'll be compelled to take it.'

Father Columba looked sadly at his brother.

Ray continued, 'I think my path is to walk alongside Ellen, to understand the difficulties that she's been through. I don't want other young ladies to go through the same difficulties. We think so alike. I think I can save her and help other young ladies too.'

Father Columba was about to say something, when looking over his brother's shoulder he saw a crucifix, where Jesus hanged to die, and he remembered that on either side of Jesus, on the two other crosses, were two convicted criminals, but only the Good Thief was repentant.

Did Jesus not teach forgiveness? Who was he to know better than God and his intentions? Bravely, Father Columba turned to his brother, hugged him, and said, 'Ray if you feel that this is your path, then walk it with your whole heart.'

The two brothers looked at each other. Ray had a tear in his eye as he said, 'I needed you to understand.'

In that moment, Father Columba felt sure his little brother had found his calling in life and his life partner: in the first prostitute that he had saved from the streets of Bolton.

10. LADY MAYFAIR'S DAUGHTER-IN-LAW

Bee woke up with a start and looked around her in confusion. She had no idea where she was. The room was large and stately, she was in a four-poster bed between cool, white, linen sheets, her head resting on cool, linen pillows. The winter sun filtered around the edges of the thick, brocade curtains that ran from floor to ceiling.

Rubbing her bruised forehead under her strawberry-blonde curls, the events of the evening before started to come back to her.

Bee had been staying with friends over Christmas in Devon, and she was going to head to her parents' house in Gloucestershire for New Year, before heading back home to London where she worked as a marketing executive. Her friends had rented out an old farmhouse for Christmas, and they had had a lot of fun. But the farmhouse was on top of a high point in the area, called Posbury Clump. Stupidly she'd decided that rather than take the short road, across to the dual carriageway, she would leave by Crediton and buy some delicious chocolates from the delicatessen for her mum, as recommended by the farmer next door.

In the twilight and the cold, Bee had steered her little car down the road from the clump. The single lane was covered in snow, and the passing vehicles had made narrow, smoothed train tracks in the road, which had frozen solid into mini toboggan runs.

Bee had managed to make it down the first decline, and cautiously she drove along an intermittent flat area, before facing the next hill. The signpost indicated right, it said "Newton's Steep". It couldn't be that bad, could it? Bee indicated right and just as she peeked over the crest of the hill, below her, in the failing light of day and emphasised by her car headlights, she saw a terrifying ski slope for cars. At the bottom was a T-junction, and opposite the steep was a big field with a river at the bottom.

Bee managed to jam her car into the hedge before she went flying down the road and pinged out the other side.

Getting out of her car, Bee slipped over on the ice and bumped her head, hard. She could feel her heart thumping out of her chest in fear. Rubbing her bruised head, she looked around for help, but no one was crazy enough to be out on a night like this.

In the dark and cold, Bee shivered as she managed to walk a little way back to the junction she'd taken. Thankfully, a kind old lady in a Land Rover, who was driving halfway up the hedge for grip, stopped to see if Bee needed help. She took pity on poor Bee, and offered her a spare room for the night, assuring her that one of her farmers would pull Bee's car out, and bring it back to the yard.

'Are you sure?' Bee asked hesitantly. 'Are you sure you can squeeze me in?'

The old lady smiled and patted her arm, 'No trouble at all, I've lots of spare rooms.'

* * *

Hesitantly, Bee stepped out of bed. She was wearing men's stripy pyjamas, which hung off her slim frame. At the end of her bed, on the padded bench, sat her clothes from the day before. They were neatly cleaned and pressed.

Bee wandered over to the window and pulling back the curtains a little way, she looked out onto the ornate, Italianate, snow-covered gardens. It was like she'd stepped into a winter paradise. Bee shook her head with the ostentatious craziness of it, then pulled back the curtains fully, to let the winter light into the room, and quickly dressed.

In the en suite, Bee found a spare toothbrush and toothpaste. Bee scrabbled around in her handbag and did the best she could with her makeup, to cover the bruise on her forehead, and wake up her hazel eyes.

Bee had a sinking feeling about her car. She could still hear the crunch as she'd run it into the hedge last night. All her bags and presents for her family were in it. But, she consoled herself, the car was

in the middle of nowhere, and if she'd had difficulty driving along the roads, then burglars were
going to have the same trouble. Hopefully, her bags
would be all right.

Bee slowly opened the heavy, oak door and
peered out. Quietly, she stepped along the landing and descended the wide, grand, sweeping oak
staircase to the checkerboard-floored hall below.

The hallway was flanked by old, oak panels.
Above the panels, on the painted silk walls, were
family pictures, some were obviously hundreds of
years old. There were also grandfather clocks ticking out time (there seemed to be at least three).
Hearing sounds from a nearby room, Bee tiptoed
towards it. Guessing that her host, Lady Mayfair,
was inside she knocked lightly on the door.

The room was as large as most people's homes. It
had three, floor-to-ceiling length windows, which
looked out onto the snow-covered, Italianate gardens that Bee had seen from her bedroom window.

The bright winter sun shone through the large
windows. At the far end of the room was a
nine-foot-high Christmas tree. It was decorated
with gold, white, and silver baubles and ribbons,
and adorned with warm-white twinkle lights. The
bright winter sun shone through the large windows. The room was decorated in yellow, gold and
cream brocades and velvets, with a large Persian
rug over the thick, cream carpet. Most of the furniture looked antique.

The room contained three occupants: a blonde,

middle-aged, tall gentleman looking out of the window. A thin, brunette lady, who had her back to Bee. And Lady Mayfair, who looked to be in her late sixties.

Lady Mayfair had salt-and-pepper-coloured hair, which she pulled back into a tight bun; her face looked kind, it was wrinkled and tanned as if she spent her days outside. She wore a purple jumper covered by a bobbled, khaki-green, fleece gilet, over dark-red cord trousers. At her feet were two rich-brown coloured cocker spaniels. She was sat on a yellow velvet sofa, opposite the thin lady and next to a roaring open fire.

Getting up from her comfortable place by the fire, Lady Mayfair came towards the door, and brought Bee into the room saying, 'Oh do come in my dear. You must be exhausted from the events of yesterday. Come and have a cup of tea and a biscuit, I will have a breakfast tray made up for you.' Lady Mayfair tried to make everything seem okay and a little less crazy. Sweeping her arm around the room, Lady Mayfair said, 'Let me introduce my son Alfie, and his second cousin, Georgie.'

By the window stood the tall man, Alfie. He had a haystack of blonde hair, and bewitching hazel eyes with laughter lines at the edges. His face was toned and masculine, but his features were gentle and calm. He turned from looking out the window, to smile at Bee in a welcoming way.

However, Georgie was less welcoming. She stiffly turned around from her position on the sofa to appraise Bee. Looking her up and down, she smiled tightly and said, 'Oh it's always so awful when you have to walk around in two-day-old clothes isn't it? And I understand you've nearly written off your car in the snow?'

Bee looked horrified, and Lady Mayfair tried to reassure her by tapping her on the arm and saying, 'It's quite all right, one of the farmers on the estate has pulled your car out of the hedge and brought it back to the yard here.' Gently adding, 'It's a little bit damaged at the front, and we may need to wait for the garages to open, but you are more than welcome to stay with us with us for a few days, while the snow clears and the car gets fixed. Unless you have family nearby?'

Bee shook her head sadly. All her friends had left the rented farmhouse yesterday. She didn't know anyone in the area apart from the farmer who'd recommended the chocolate shop to her, and she'd only had a ten-minute conversation with him.

'I don't know anybody nearby.' Bee said worriedly. 'My friends and I rented a farmhouse for Christmas, and we all left yesterday. I was on the way to Gloucestershire, to my parents' house. A farmer told me about this amazing delicatessen in Crediton, with artisan chocolates, I was stupidly going to stop there to get some for my mum and I didn't follow my friends along the top road to the dual carriageway.' Bee shook her head and looked at her feet, cursing her bad luck. She continued, saying, 'I wish I hadn't.'

Lady Mayfair consoled her, 'Now, now. There's no point wishing for something to be undone. Besides, we're always glad of company. I don't think the snow will clear for a few days, and your car obviously needs fixing. Why don't you spend the New Year with us? You never know, perhaps it's fate?' and she smiled kindly at poor Bee.

* * *

Later that morning, Bee was able to retrieve, with the help of Alfie, her suitcases from the back of her mangled car. Surveying the damage, she shuddered in fear at the thought of the toboggan run called "Newton's Steep".

Alfie gently said to her, 'You're lucky you didn't slide down the hill. . .' He stopped talking and gave her a look, taking in her slim frame, strawberry blonde hair, hazel eyes and fine features. Bee had the distinct feeling that something bad would have happened if she hadn't crashed her car into the hedge. She shuddered again at the thought of it, and Alfie lay a reassuring hand on her shoulder as he said, 'Well I'm quite glad of your company. Besides, my mum is trying to set me up with my cousin Georgie, and I don't know if I'm ready to settle down yet. So, you may have done me a favour.' He smiled again and winked at her, as he lugged her heavy suitcases indoors, and she grabbed the last of her family's Christmas presents, to carry safely inside.

✻ ✻ ✻

Bee was given the run of the downstairs and told to "look around". So after lunch, she started exploring. At the far end of the house were the kitchens and old servant's quarters. Also, on the ground floor was a TV room, a dining room, a games room with a snooker table, a library, a study, and a sitting room, where it seemed Lady Mayfair preferred to sit with Georgie, unless Lady Mayfair was off about the estate, on the farms, or walking her dogs. Bee even explored as far as the kitchens where the housekeeper was welcoming and helpful.

Wandering back to the main hall, Bee heard somebody playing snooker in the games room. Deciding to be sociable, she tapped lightly on the door and poked her head around it.

Alfie was all alone. The snooker table was enormous and covered in multicoloured balls. Alfie appeared to be trying out trick shots. He looked delighted to have somebody to play with, and coming over to the door he ushered her in as he said, 'Have you ever played snooker?' Bee shook her head "No." as he continued, 'Well that's perfect, this is your golden opportunity.'

Alfie gave Bee his snooker cue and poured them both a generous whiskey from the drinks cabinet at the side of the room.

Alfie passed her a heavy, cut-crystal glass, and

as he did so their fingertips brushed. He looked up sharply from her glass, and their eyes connected. In that moment something changed. He went from being a stranger that she didn't know, in a large, old house, to being a kindred spirit and a connection that she couldn't do without.

They stood there, looking at each other. Bee was sure Alfie felt it too. She broke her eye connection with him and looked down at the glass of whiskey, saying in a small voice, 'Thank you, that's so kind.' She looked back up at him, to see him still staring at her.

Embarrassed, Alfie grabbed his glass and said, 'Well, cheers to you, Bee. It is lovely to meet you.'

They clinked their glasses together, and both took a sip of the sweet, fiery whiskey.

Suddenly, Bee wanted very much to just reach out and touch Alfie. It was the strangest feeling; she didn't know him at all.

Alfie fidgeted uneasily with his snooker cue and put his whiskey down announcing, 'Okay, let me show you the rules of the game.'

It was almost as if they'd entered another world. Everything outside of their bubble of two didn't exist, and time seemed to stop altogether. They spent their time together playing snooker and enjoying being around each other. Alfie seemed embarrassed when he tried to show her how to hold the cue properly, it was as if he was afraid to touch her, like there was an invisible barrier of acceptability, pushing him away.

Bee could feel the sparks flying between their two bodies, inches from each other, it was all she could do to concentrate on the game. When they made eye contact, it was as if neither of them could look away. The attraction between them was undeniable.

Darkness fell outside. Suddenly there was a loud knock on the door, and Georgie stormed in saying, 'Oh, so that's where you two have been hiding all day. Well just so you know it's nearly time for dinner.' Looking Bee up and down, Georgie turned from her and smiled at Alfie. Then she turned on her heel and left.

* * *

Bee put on a dress for dinner. She had a feeling it was the sort of place where you "got dressed for dinner". She chose a black velvet, cowl back, midi-dress from her suitcase. Thankfully she was correct in her assumption.

Bee came down to the sitting room (with the Christmas tree and roaring fire) before dinner. She found Georgie and Alfie talking, comfortably sat on the yellow velvet sofas in front of the fire. Alfie jumped up as if he'd been stung when Bee entered, and immediately rushed to get her a drink. Bee followed his suggestion of a whiskey with a dash of water, and Bee sat down beside Georgie on the sofa, opposite Alfie's spot, as he handed her the heavy, cut-crystal glass.

Georgie smiled tightly, and shuffled along the sofa, away from Bee and closer to the fire.

Bee started to feel uncomfortable. She placed her bag on the sofa next to her, took a big sip of whiskey, and tried not to splutter at the fieriness of it.

Alfie sat back down again, opposite them both. He said, 'I can see I must be the luckiest guy alive, to be spending an evening with two such beautiful women.'

Georgie grabbed the compliments where she could and immediately exclaimed, 'Alfie you're just the best, calling me beautiful.' She fluttered her eyelashes at him.

Bee briefly made eye contact, and gently shook her head to bat the compliment away. Just as before, Bee felt a magnetic pull towards Alfie. She could tell by the way he "danced" to entertain them both, that he was feeling it too.

Lady Mayfair joined them in the sitting room, and the four of them went through to the dining room for dinner. Alfie made sure that he sat himself next to Bee at the dinner table. The chemistry between them was undeniable.

Over dinner, Lady Mayfair talked about the estate and the family. She had been widowed for five years, and Alfie was their only son. The estate was large and focussed on farming. Common with many old estates, it was desperately in need of an injection of funds. The plan was for Alfie to leave his banking job in the city and return to run the family estate.

Georgiana, his second cousin, was the daughter of Mr Fleet who owned half the newspapers in London. It appeared that Georgie's mum had married very well, and Georgie was very rich. Bee understood now why Lady Mayfair wanted Alfie and Georgie to hit it off. It seemed that Georgie's appearance down here with Alfie and Lady Mayfair over New Year, when the estate was needing a large injection of cash, wasn't a mistake. In fact, Bee would go so far as to say she had the feeling that Lady Mayfair was hoping Alfie would propose to Georgie, despite Alfie telling her he wasn't ready to settle down. It was clear that Bee was not part of their plan.

After dinner, Lady Mayfair and Georgie played card games in front of the fire, and seizing his opportunity, Alfie suggested that Bee come and join him in the games room to play snooker.

Georgie stopped shuffling the cards mid-shuffle and looked annoyed. Lady Mayfair looked sharply up and said, 'Alfie darling, after you finish your game, do come and play cards with Georgie.'

Alfie replied, 'Of course.' Then smiling at Georgie he said, 'I'll be right back to play cards with you after my game.' Having appeased this mother, he ducked out of the room, taking Bee along with him.

The touch of his hand was like putting her fingers in a plug socket. Bee was electrified and overwhelmed. She didn't want to let go. Alfie pulled her through into the games room, where he put the lights on and pushed the door nearly closed behind them. Turning to her, he slowly let go of her hand and they stood facing each other, not more than half a foot apart. Alfie was breathing heavily and her breathing matched his.

Alfie said, 'This is crazy, I haven't been able to stop thinking about you all day. I know I've only just met you, and this is the maddest thing I've ever said, can I kiss you?'

Bee was overwhelmed. She felt the same. This couldn't be happening? Nodding slowly, she looked deeply into his eyes as he leant down, and his mouth connected with hers.

Alfie's lips were as soft as marshmallows. As he gently moved against her, the smell of a spicy, woody aftershave filled her nose. He smelt of security and strength, excitement and adventure. Alfie grew more confident in their kiss. His hand moved along her shoulder and up into her hair. His other hand reached around her back as he pulled her towards him.

Bee felt dazed, as if she was being transported to another world. It was almost as if she was in some sort of fairy tale, and she'd just met her Prince Charming. This couldn't be happening to her, could it? She didn't belong here. Georgie and her money did. This wasn't right, Bee didn't belong.

With a herculean effort, Bee pulled back from the kiss, and pushed Alfie back away saying, 'I can't do this, I don't belong here, we're from different worlds.' She shook her head sadly, to try and emphasise the point, and stepped back further, forcing Alfie to let her go.

Not willing to lose her, Alfie stretched out his hand, to try to take her hand in his. Barely holding her fingertips, he said, 'I know you feel it too. I saw it in your eyes. I know you feel the same way about me, as I feel about you.'

Bee just shook her head and looked down at her feet before saying, 'Alfie, Georgie is here because your mum wants you to marry her. Isn't she?'

Alfie let go of her hand and he looked away from her, slowly running his hands over his face and through his stack of golden hair.

'Isn't she?' Bee insisted.

Not looking at Bee, Alfie said in a small voice, 'Yes. Mum wants me to marry her. I don't love her.' He turned back to face Bee. 'And until today, I think I probably would have done it, but for some strange reason, it seems that Father Christmas has sent me you. You've changed everything.'

'Alfie, I've just met you. It's not right. You think a stranger can save you from this, but I can't. You have to make your own decisions. You shouldn't be forced into marriage, but equally, you shouldn't be looking at me as an escape. Perhaps your feelings for me are just about escaping and that's all.'

Alfie hit the side of the snooker table, 'That's not the way I feel, and you know it.'

'Alfie, I've only just met you.'

'How can I convince you of the way I feel about you, about us?' Alfie had a good idea that she felt the same way about him. He could feel it when he was around her and by the way they looked at each other.

Bee wanted nothing more than to be next to Alfie, always. But she had to be sure she wasn't going to lose herself in a fairy tale. Musing on what he'd said, she replied, 'Well, it looks like my car won't be fixed until the New Year due to the heavy snow and getting the replacement car parts, so I give you a week. Your mum has kindly allowed me to stay. You have a week to convince me this is how you really feel and I'm not just an escape for you. Deal?'

Alfie came towards Bee, and pulled her towards him saying, 'Deal. Whatever I have to do to convince you, I will do it.' He looked down at her as if he was about to kiss her again.

The old, oak door started to creak open, and Bee and Alfie sprang apart as Georgie came in. She looked suspiciously at them and said, 'Oh I see you haven't started your game of snooker yet? Perhaps I can join you?'

Alfie took control of the situation saying, 'Yes, come and join us Georgie, we can take turns rotating, each game.'

Georgie looked slyly at Bee as she said, 'I love winning at snooker.' She went to the stand to select herself a cue.

❊ ❊ ❊

The three of them played snooker late into the night. Lady Mayfair came in at a few points, and looked on delightedly, making eye contact significantly with Alfie.

Bee felt even more awkward knowing that it was Lady Mayfair's desire that Georgie and Alfie get engaged. Bee was the other woman, the unexpected guest. The person Lady Mayfair had extended her hospitality to. Suddenly everything seemed very mixed up.

Later that evening, Bee was glad to get back to the quiet of her own room and check her text messages. She could still feel Alfie's lips against hers. She tried to shake the thought and managed a quick call to her parents to update them.

Her parents were worried initially, however, after Bee explained, they were just glad that she was safe, and that someone kind was looking after her. Bee was concerned because heavy snow was still forecast for the next four days, and by the time her car was fixed and the roads were cleared of snow she would likely have very little time with her parents before returning to work in London. However, her parents assured her that she could always come for a long weekend in the spring, and the main thing was, she was safe.

❊ ❊ ❊

Now that Alfie had been given the challenge to win Bee over, he focussed intently on it. Somehow, he seemed to engineer situations where Georgie was running around after his mum and caught up in estate matters. While he carved out chunks of time with Bee, by taking her on snowy walks on the estate.

Bee had equipped herself well for a Christmas in the country. She had a snowsuit, fur-lined wellies, a fur-lined deerstalker hat, and woolly gloves. The cold air gave her face a fresh, healthy look; with a pink tinge to her cheeks and nose. Her hazel eyes sparkled in the winter sunlight, and her straw-berry-blonde curls escaped from under her deer-stalker hat. Every day Alfie would think of new places to walk with her. He spent the time talking to her, listening to her, and asking her questions. It seemed he had a high-profile job in the city. They compared notes on London, finding that they lived at opposite ends of the city and didn't know any-one in common.

During the day on New Year's Eve, Alfie sug-gested they walk to the folly and look at the hermit's cave on the way.

Several hundred years ago, a resident hermit had lived on the estate, refusing to interact with any-one, unless they brought him food. In return, he gave pieces of wisdom and advice. The sort of advice that comes to you after refusing to talk to anyone for years and forcefully putting yourself in solitary confinement. Bee inspected the cave, which appeared to be little more than a small, ex-cavated hole, at one of the far-flung reaches of the wild gardens. Her heart pounded when Alfie followed her in and lit her way with his phone, but he was the perfect gentleman.

Alfie took them along a tree-lined vista, where a Grecian-looking temple stood at the far end of the line of trees. The folly looked back onto the estate in one direction, and out over the countryside in the other.

When they reached the folly, Bee discovered that it was a single circular room, about five metres high, surrounded by a circle of skinny stone pillars, with a stone dome on top.

Bee and Alfie walked around the building. At each of the four compass points, there was a little stone seat, placed between the inner room and the pillars. Sitting down, they looked out over the wintry landscape spread before them. It was as if the world had been scrubbed clean by ice-white snow. Small snowflakes continued to gently fall from the brooding grey sky above them. A light wind caught the falling snowflakes causing them to dance and swirl in the breeze. Bee felt as if she was in an enchanted other world. They sat on the stone bench looking out, content in each other's company, not needing to say a word.

Through her gloves, Alfie took Bee's hand and placed it between his own. He cleared his throat and said, 'You know Bee, connections like this happen once in a lifetime if you're lucky. I know you don't believe me. All I can do is just keep asking you to let me in. I don't know how else to do this.' He lifted her gloved hand to his lips and kissed it. He met her eyes and said, 'You know that it's you that I want, don't you?' Alfie leant forward and gently kissed her. Their bodies drew together as if they were the only two people who existed in the world.

Alfie was exactly who Bee wanted. She wanted the smell of him and the feel of him. She melted at his touch. She wanted her hand in his hand, his arms around her. But, she didn't want to be a homewrecker and she didn't want to upset Lady Mayfair who had kindly given her shelter when she needed it most. Bee also didn't want to wake up and find this was all some strange dream. But for the moment, she let her body succumb to his kisses and she allowed herself to open to his lips.

Alfie pulled back a little and looked, dazed, into her eyes saying, 'There you are, I knew you were there, I knew you felt the same.'

Bee said, 'Alfie, your family estate needs money and I am not rich. If we're together it is likely that you will lose all of this.'

Flippantly, Alfie said, 'I don't care. It's you I want. I have to have you.' Leaning forward, he kissed her again.

* * *

For New Year's Eve, Bee wore the same black velvet dress as the first evening. When she came down to dinner, she found Alfie in a dinner jacket and both ladies in glittery dresses.

The atmosphere at dinner was a little strange. Because it was New Year's Eve, everybody wanted to be jolly and in good spirits. Lady Mayfair had made sure there was plenty of champagne so that they could spend the evening celebrating. But Georgie was decidedly annoyed at once again getting fobbed off with Alfie's mother and not Alfie. Even worse, the chemistry between Bee and Alfie was undeniable. They hardly dared to look at each other. Alfie was constantly checking to see if Georgie noticed and Bee felt like an imposter around Lady Mayfair.

After dinner, they adjourned to the sitting room and Lady Mayfair put on some jazz music. Collectively they played cards together at the table in front of the fire, as they waited for their guests to arrive.

It was traditional that on New Year's Eve, all the workers from the estate were invited to the house, to join the family for the evening, and see in the new year. By about nine p.m. the room was full of at least twenty people, all in their Sunday best.

The dynamic had changed significantly, and far from the suspicious glances and hidden secrets over dinner, everybody was genuinely jolly, happy and excited to welcome in the new year and hoping it would be better than the last. There were a lot of conversations about the estate and plans for next year.

Lady Mayfair was in her element, making sure that everybody was attended to with drinks and making everybody feel included. Bee looked over guiltily, she really was a kind woman. Tonight, she showed to her guests the same kindness she had shown Bee when she'd taken her in. Bee took a sip of champagne and thought guiltily about all the times that she and Alfie had kissed. She felt as if she was destroying it all.

Georgie spent the evening trying to do her best to emulate Lady Mayfair, but she was a poor imitation, and her efforts came off somewhere between sarcastic and insincere. Wherever Georgie was, Alfie appeared to be at the opposite side of the room, and always trying to get back to Bee.

Bee enjoyed talking to the estate workers, finding out what they did and trying to understand a little bit more about how the estate worked.

Unlike many stately homes, the estate didn't open to the public or advertise itself as a stately home for visitors. Instead, it tried to make its money through farming, and although it was holding its own, there were areas which needed large amounts of cash.

Bee looked over at Alfie. She knew he worked in city banking, and that he was good at his job, but could he make enough to save the estate without Georgie's help?

* * *

Midnight drew closer and people started talking about their resolutions for the next year, how they wanted to be better, what they were going to do on the estate, and what changes they wanted in their lives.

Bee thought about her life and what she wanted. If she could choose freely, she would choose to be with Alfie, without a doubt. Bee looked over at Alfie, and she knew that if he could choose freely, he would choose to be with her. Bee looked at Georgie, and she knew that Georgie wanted Alfie too, and that made her feel uncomfortable. Bee looked at Lady Mayfair and knew that if Lady Mayfair could choose her best year next year, it would be that the estate made money and that they could do the essential repairs they needed, to keep things ticking over.

In the corner of the room, somebody turned on the radio and a slight hush descended as everybody expectantly waited for the countdown to midnight. Joining in with the radio presenter, the happy crowd counted down to the New Year and waited for the bells of Big Ben to sound out over the airwaves, before cheering, congratulating each other, holding hands and singing out, 'Auld Lang Syne'.

Alfie had made sure that he was next to Bee, and squeezing her hand, he looked down at her as he said the words, 'We'll tak' a cup o' kindness yet,' Bee couldn't help but look at him back and smile.

As the song finished, everybody congratulated each other again on the start of the new year, and hugged and kissed, wishing each other well.

Alfie whispered to Bee, 'If I don't do this now, I will lose my confidence, and I never will.'

In the middle of the room, Alfie got down on one knee and said, 'Bee, will you do me the honour of becoming my wife?'

* * *

The room was like a melting pot about to explode. Most of the guests thought that this was the perfect start to the new year and excitedly waited for her answer. Lady Mayfair held her hand over her mouth in shock, and Georgie was so angry she looked as if she might murder somebody.

In that moment, Bee recognised Alfie's bravery, and knowing she had completely fallen for him, she shut the world out, looked deeply into his eyes and said, 'Yes.'

The bomb exploded. The room erupted into clapping, and estate workers came to congratulate the happy couple. Most assumed Alfie had met Bee in London. Georgie left the room; her face was as black as a thundercloud. Lady Mayfair hid her feelings well, and stoically came over to congratulate her son and her new daughter-in-law. Lady Mayfair had had no idea Alfie had fallen for Bee, and she'd thought her plan of Alfie and Georgie falling in love, or at least getting acquainted, had been going well. She was in complete shock and blindsided by Alfie's choice.

Eventually, the guests started to say their goodbyes and leave. Lady Mayfair graciously wished them a, "Happy New Year." Bee lost her courage and said goodnight as she retired for bed too. Alfie was about to retire himself, when Lady Mayfair asked him to stay back with her a little while.

There was nothing Bee could do. This was a conversation to which she was not invited. Alfie had to make his own decisions. However, she still felt guilty. Lady Mayfair had taken her in, and she had returned the favour by stealing her son's heart and destroying the financial prospects of the estate.

Alfie was risking it all for her.

Shakily, Bee ascended the stairs to the cool calm of her enormous bedroom. Quickly washing and changing, Bee slipped into bed.

* * *

Not more than half an hour later there was a gentle tap on Bee's bedroom door. Bee had been lying awake, terrified of the conversation Alfie was having with his mother. She was also buzzing with the realisation that she was engaged to a man she'd met a week ago. Her parents would think she was mad. She hadn't the confidence to tell them, yet. They wouldn't understand. Bee's relationship with Alfie seemed magnetic and intense. Alfie was like a fairy prince, living in a castle.

Bee switched on the bedside lamp as the tap came again. Bee cautiously slipped out of bed and padded over to the large, oak door. Opening it ajar she peered out. There was Alfie, still in his dinner jacket, smiling confidently at her. He looked intently into her eyes and said, 'Can I come in?'

Bee bit her lip, and pulled back the door slightly, allowing him to enter. Closing the door behind them, she turned to him and said, 'Alfie you're risking it all for me.'

Alfie smiled a slightly cocky smile and said, 'I've always been pretty good at gambling. I have weighed up the odds. I need to have a stellar year at work this year If I'm going to keep you and the estate. Mum doesn't think I can do it, but now that I have the incentive, I know that I can.'

Bee looked up into Alfie's eyes. She admired his bravery. Reaching out her hand, she took his hand and said, 'I know it must be something that you've thought of before, but tonight I talked to a lot of your employees on the estate. . . You know I'm very good at marketing? Well, I think I might be able to do something to help you, I think you should open the house as a wedding venue this year, I think you will make quite a lot of money.'

Alfie looked down adoringly at her, and smiled saying, 'I knew there was a reason why Father Christmas gifted you to me.'

Alfie stepped towards her, he took her in his arms and kissed her, passionately. All their pent-up desire came pouring out. Every kiss this week was as if they'd been handcuffed. Now they were free. Free to touch, free to connect. Their hearts rose high on emotion, Bee felt her body tingle as Alfie ran his hands over her. A week ago, she'd felt as if she was in some strange fairy tale. Right now, she didn't want to be anywhere else in the world. Next to Alfie was where she belonged.

Alfie drew away from their kiss and took off his dinner jacket, dropping it to the floor, before pulling Bee towards him. Kissing her again.

11. DARLING, I PROMISE I WILL BE HOME FOR CHRISTMAS

It was a week until Christmas and it was Gerald's last business trip. He hated being away from home so close to Christmas; he loved the house when his children and wife were excited and getting ready for the festive season. He loved watching them wrapping presents and making delicious cakes and pies; while he ate good food, next to the fire with his dog at his feet, holding a dram of whiskey, scrolling the news and generally being doted on. Bliss. Instead, he was stuck in Munich, in a cubic, soulless hotel room, attending silly meetings with people that just expounded the same point again and again, and nothing got decided upon. Gerald particularly hated spending a *weekend* away while he sorted the last of his company's business.

The city was cold and damp, and slushy and snowy. Everybody seemed to have somebody, but his people were far away.

Gerald flicked away a bit of slush from his Italian leather shoe, as he wandered aimlessly along the pavement in the cold evening. Christmas decorations adorned the shops and busy shoppers pushed on by. He was bored and he was getting battered trying to walk against the merry tide. It was just when he'd decided to go back to the hotel, that he passed the jeweller's window, and the necklace caught his eye.

It was a sleek, sparkly, blue-enamelled, periwinkle flower set with a gold chain. Gerald had listened to his wife talk about her childhood necklace her dad had given her a hundred times, and how sad she was that she'd lost it when she'd moved out after university. Gerald's wife always thought that he wasn't listening, but that wasn't true, he always listened and he always heard, he just didn't often answer. Instead, he took it all in.

It seemed a little bit too much like fate had put the necklace in the window before him on purpose. Gerald had already got his wife a very nice cashmere dressing gown, but he just knew this necklace was meant for her. He entered the jewellery shop with a little *ping* to announce his arrival.

❊ ❊ ❊

Gerald nodded in sympathy as his wife moaned down the phone at him. His black, now greying, hair was slicked back in neat waves over his head. His thick black-and-grey eyebrows rose and lowered gently over his unusual grey eyes, with each new wave of his wife's conversation. He didn't disagree with her. He wished he was there too. But

223

what could he do? He had to provide for them all. He was also proud and satisfied with what he'd achieved, although being away in the run-up to Christmas wasn't exactly a perk of the job. Gerald wished dearly he was at home being moaned at instead.

His wife's voice rose a little, he could almost see her pink, soft lips narrowing and her hands on her hips, emphasising her figure. She said, 'So, when do you think you will be back?'

Gerald sighed. She didn't understand. He wanted to come home. Calmly he replied, 'Some key issues need to get resolved before I leave Munich and get back to headquarters. I think it's just a delay of a day. It means I'll be travelling back on the evening of the 23 December, so I'll be back for Christmas Eve.' Gerald wiped his muscly, tanned hand over the brow of his forehead, and tried to relax back into the hard hotel chair.

His wife huffed angrily. Gerald could almost see her thin eyebrows crunching together over her fine-featured, petite face and her soft, blonde curls, lightly bouncing around her head as she shook it in annoyance. She stated, 'But this is very inconvenient. I don't like it at all. I don't like you flying back so close to Christmas.'

Gerald replied with the fateful words, 'Darling, I promise I will be home for Christmas.' He really did mean it.

* * *

The talks were frustrating and nothing seemed to get resolved quickly. Gerald was mild-mannered, never doing more than raising his eyebrows or asking politely to resolve a point again. Finally, on the afternoon of the 23 December they managed to reach an agreement, and Gerald was able to call headquarters to confirm his work was done. Gratefully, he returned to his box hotel room. Carefully, he checked the little, blue, periwinkle flower necklace in its red, cushioned box, one more time, then stowed it away in his laptop bag. He closed his laptop, put it away, and packed the last of his belongings to depart for the airport.

The snow was building up on the pavement outside, and Gerald shivered in his navy-blue, wool Crombie as he waited for his taxi. When the taxi arrived, the doorman helpfully placed his suitcase in the boot and opened the back door of the taxi for Gerald.

Gerald tried to push back the excitement that had been building in his tummy. He was going home. With the little German that Gerald spoke, he asked to go to the airport and gave the terminal number. With the little German that Gerald understood, he was sure that the taxi driver was making comments about the weather, expounded by expressive hand gestures. Gerald nodded and smiled kindly. Taking out his phone he replied to some urgent work emails.

* * *

The airport was very busy. Dusk had fallen along with another dump of snow, and there were taxis, people, cars and suitcases everywhere. Gerald hated travelling during the chaos of Christmas, but at least his work was done, and he was finally getting to go home to be with his family. After all, that's what Christmas was about for him. Not the presents, just the comfort of being around his family.

Gerald was travelling business class and took a fast-track lane through to the check-in counter for his suitcase. It dawned on him there were a few issues. He looked up to the departures board to see lots of red, flashing delays. The lady at the check-in desk confirmed the sinking feeling in his tummy; the planes were delayed. The snow was a little heavier than he'd realised and the bad weather was continuing to come in. Still, he managed to check in his suitcase, and that was the first hurdle over.

Gerald carefully stowed his precious boarding pass into his breast pocket and went through passport control. He could feel himself unwinding a little from the chaos of the airport as he passed into the gold star, exclusive, business lounge. There were soft, buttery, leather chairs and sofas, with side tables and reading lamps dotted about. Green faux ferns in raised planters were used to divide the space, and at the far end was a food counter and a dining area. More to distract himself than feeling hungry, Gerald wandered over to the buffet bar to see what calorific foods he could abuse his body with, and shut out the gnawing fear of delays.

Gerald helped himself to chicken korma, naan bread, and rice; and a large slice of apple strudel and cream for pudding. The gold star lounge dining area was quite full (he wasn't the only passenger eating away their sorrows) so he had to share a table with a young lady called Miriam. They spoke briefly about work and what rotten weather it was. She was travelling back to Manchester too, and they both looked sadly out onto the runways; which were full of planes, airport personnel, baggage trucks and slush on the ground. More snowflakes fluttered down to join the fun. It was a perfect mess. There was nothing either of them could do, they just had to trust the process.

* * *

Gerald and the young lady, Miriam, spent a very pleasant hour together over dinner. Their flight had been delayed further. Usually, Gerald would be frustrated internally, wishing things would move along a bit or that he could get behind the scenes and organise the process better (Gerald was good at that) but in Miriam's light company, he found that he wasn't as annoyed as usual, and the time passed quickly, as the delay signs pinged up like popcorn on the departures board.

Gerald studied his companion. Miriam had the same style of blonde hair as his wife; falling in similar soft curls, although Miriam had scooped most of it up at the back, with only a few little face-framing curls escaping. She had sparkling blue eyes; a lightly tanned and freckled, round face; and a neat, little nose. She wore a nondescript, grey, business suit, and like him had a serviceable coat and briefcase. Miriam worked in food distribution, and just like him she was hoping to get home for Christmas; to get back to her parents' house, to be with family and celebrate. They both compared notes on family Christmas traditions and talked easily about some of the difficulties of business negotiation and strategy.

Gerald looked over to the departures board. He could see that their flight to Manchester was already delayed by over two hours. He looked out of the window. Despite promises from the airport staff that the flight would take off tonight, he could see that it was looking increasingly snowy outside and the window of opportunity to escape Munich before Christmas seemed to be getting smaller. Gerald turned his head back to Miriam to continue the conversation. He didn't want to worry her.

Luckily, just before eleven, while they were enjoying a second post-dinner glass of champagne, the gate for their flight was finally announced. Gerald good-naturedly helped Miriam on with her coat and they walked together to the gate. There was another small delay at the gate, but not more than twenty minutes, and then they were boarding. Finally.

First class on the plane was little more than the advantage of being sat at the front of the plane and having a small curtain divide between your group and everybody else. It didn't shut out the noise and the seat space wasn't any different. Possibly there were more snacks and better alcohol, but Gerald wasn't a big drinker.

Sadly, Miriam was a few seats away, across the aisle, and so Gerald wasn't able to continue his conversation with her. In fact, the plane was quite full. Gerald was starting to feel a bit hemmed in. He reached into his briefcase and took out his laptop. Inside his bag sat the little, red velvet box with the periwinkle necklace in it. Carefully, he took it out and had a little peek. He felt good knowing how excited his wife would be. Gerald smiled. Gently replacing the flower necklace, he worked his way through yet another report on his laptop. Politely, Gerald added comments to the margin and saved the document to send back to the unsuccessful team leader tomorrow.

Half an hour had passed and they hadn't moved. Gerald looked out of his window, down onto the slushy tarmac outside, and thought of home. His wife had had the neighbours around for drinks that evening. She always held a small party the night before Christmas Eve. He'd missed it. Christmas Eve at home was a last crazy dash of wrapping presents while she listened to her favourite jazz Christmas music in the background. There would be freshly cooked, mince pies with clotted cream, and leftovers from the drinks party, such as little fancy pastries, carrot sticks and houmous. Gerald would do a few light jobs (like walking the dog), but mainly he liked to sit in his chair with a dram of whiskey and absorb the happy sounds of his wife and two daughters. He could see it now: the house was warm and tastefully decorated by his lovely wife; with modern Christmas decorations and twinkling lights. The tree was her triumph as every year she picked a different theme. It made her so happy. Gerald smiled at the thought. His little man cave of a study... *thump.*

Gerald's eyes flicked open as the man in the seat next to him accidentally bopped him on the head with his briefcase. Gerald looked around. Instead of home, he was bunched up with a lot of grumpy strangers in a metal tin with wheels.

Gerald sighed and looked back out of the window to see more snow fall on the runway and people dashing around. Baggage trolleys were making slushy tracks in the snow, and aeroplanes were sitting in their bays, not moving. Gerald checked the time on his phone. The flight should've left over half an hour ago. In fact, he should've been in Manchester long ago. He'd texted his wife but didn't say much because he didn't want to worry her. Besides she'd been busy with the party and he was going to be getting a taxi back home, so she wouldn't be waiting up for him.

Across the aisle, Gerald could see that Miriam

was also looking depressed as she watched the chaos out the window. At that very moment, she turned around and caught his eye. She smiled weakly, in an exasperated sort of way, and he smiled and nodded back. It was funny, how fate throws you together with strangers in the most frustrating of circumstances.

* * *

They were off! After a four-hour delay. It was going to be after midnight before they landed in Manchester. Gerald breathed a sigh of relief. Pilots were experts at navigating bad weather.

Gerald remembered back to when they'd bought their current home. His two little girls were still waist height, and his wife had been just as beautiful as she was now. She'd picked the house, obviously, and he'd paid for it. It was a nineteen-thirties, suburban, detached, four-bedroom house; a mixture of white plaster and red bricks. It had a wide arched porch, beautiful bay windows and large airy rooms inside. He smiled. His wife had worked her magic on the décor; the rooms were painted in soft creams and whites, picked out by spots of bright oranges and teals in the soft furnishings and wall art. Home.

Gerald let his hand reach into the briefcase to touch the small red box inside. Carefully removing it, he took another peek at the blue, periwinkle flower necklace. He carefully replaced the little red box and pulled out his laptop. He didn't feel much like doing work at the moment, but there was no point ignoring it.

* * *

Gerald realised there were more problems to come somewhere over the East Coast of England. Firstly because of the turbulence, and secondly because the pilot spoke over the Tannoy to announce they were going to have to divert to Birmingham. It was past midnight and Birmingham Airport wasn't exactly convenient. Gerald took a glance over at Miriam, she turned to look at him and raised her eyebrows in a shared code between them.

The weary passengers made their way to the baggage carousel to collect bags which were being unceremoniously chucked off the plane. Gerald had been offered accommodation in Birmingham tonight, and a taxi back to Manchester later. But Gerald just wanted to push on and get home. He stood by the baggage carousel, waiting for his battered suitcase to appear. The Christmas spirit was starting to wear thin.

'Hello stranger!' a sweet voice beside him said. Gerald turned to see the pretty smile of Miriam and her sparkling blue eyes. Despite the long journey she still seemed cheerful.

Gerald smiled back and said, 'You're still so upbeat? We've had such a difficult flight and a long wait. You must have a lot of patience.'

'Well, I guess there's not much we can do is there? Just go with the flow. At least we're back in the UK. For a moment I thought I was going to be spending Christmas in Munich with you.' Miriam smiled and her eyes fluttered prettily. Suddenly, out of the corner of her eye, she spotted her suitcase. Lurching forward she tried to grab it. Ever the gentleman, Gerald leapt into action and managed to retrieve it before it went on another loop of the carousel. Gerald passed it to her.

'Thank you so much.' Miriam gratefully replied and blushed slightly. 'Hey, are you travelling to Manchester? Do you want to get a taxi with me?' her voice trembled slightly.

Gerald smiled, 'What a good idea. Let's travel together.' He put his briefcase strap over his shoulder, grabbed both suitcases, and they exited the airport to try and find a taxi in the middle of the Christmas airport chaos.

❋ ❋ ❋

The queue looked as if it was at least a hundred people long. The problem with business class is it doesn't get you anywhere when you're waiting in a queue for a taxi. Nobody cares if your company is paying. Nobody cares if you want to get home to your family, because everybody else wants to get home to their family too.

Gerald and Miriam chatted amicably. He was glad to have found a travelling companion; it distracted him from thoughts of home.

At two in the morning, cold and tired, they neared the front of the queue and watched a few solitary taxis merry-go-round into the taxi bay. Most people weren't going into Birmingham. Most people wanted to get home for Christmas, so they were either connecting to train stations (ready for the first trains later in the morning) or they were getting taxis to their final destinations, and the taxis weren't coming back any time soon.

Gerald and Miriam were so glad of a taxi they took what they got. It was a tired-looking car driven by a tired-looking man. The taxi driver helped them with their bags, and Gerald and Miriam both took their briefcases into the back with them. The driver had put a little bit of tinsel around his mirror and was playing some ancient Christmas pop songs on the radio. It seemed like a half-hearted attempt for the customers at some Christmas spirit.

Gerald politely said, 'Let's drop you off first, and then we'll go to my stop.'

Miriam touched him gently on the arm. 'Are you sure?' she said, kindly looking up from under her thick, full lashes.

Gerald smiled graciously. 'I'm absolutely sure. Besides, the family will all be asleep, they won't notice what time I come in.' He clicked his seatbelt into its holder and touched the bump in his laptop bag where the necklace lay safely in its box. Miriam gave the taxi driver her address and Gerald gave the driver his, instructing him to drop Miriam off first.

Miriam continued to make light conversation. 'So, you said you had a wife and daughters?'

'Yes! I don't know how my wife puts up with me, but she does. She's very good to all of us. We are very fond of each other. In fact, I've got her the perfect Christmas present.'

Miriam raised her eyebrows and said, 'Oh, you really have cracked it then!' and looked on expectantly.

Gerald reached into his briefcase and pulled out the little red box. In the semi-darkness, he switched on the torch on his phone. He opened the box to show Miriam the periwinkle-flower necklace. The blue enamel shone in the darkness.

'Oh! It's quite beautiful.' Miriam said enviously, as she eyed up the gift. 'Your wife will be delighted, I know.'

Gerald smiled and snapped the box shut with satisfaction. 'Yes, she will. It's just like the one her father got her when she was little. When I saw it in the shop window in Munich, I just knew it was waiting for me to buy it for her. I didn't even haggle the jeweller down. I suspect the jeweller knows he got a good deal.' Gerald shook his head good-naturedly and carefully replaced the box in his briefcase.

As they came towards Manchester, they found that there had been an accident on the motorway and a diversion was set up that took them nearer to Gerald's house than Miriam's. The taxi driver suggested that Gerald was dropped off first. He seemed like a decent man, so Miriam insisted that it was a better plan. Gerald could see it was the most sensible thing to do (and he was glad to be getting home finally) so he agreed as long as he paid the entire fare.

The diversion took them down some back roads, which were as pot-holed as an army obstacle course. The car thumped through some nasty bumps. It was nearly four in the morning and quite dark. No one else was taking the diversion. The car hit a particularly nasty bump and all three occupants gave a collective, "Oh!" as the taxi driver skidded to a slushy, snowy stop, at a pull-in at the edge of the road.

Miriam looked around nervously as the driver got out to check the car. Gerald had a bad feeling about this. It seemed like fate was doing everything it could to stop him from getting home. The driver popped his head back in and said, 'Sorry, it's a flat. I've got a spare in the back. Give me ten minutes and I'll quickly change it.'

'Let me help you.' Gerald insisted.

'Nah, it's all right mate. I used to work as a mechanic. It won't take me a jiffy.'

Gerald nodded his acknowledgement of the driver's superior competency and let him get on with the job.

Miriam and Gerald sat in the back of the taxi while the taxi driver started jacking up the car.

Miriam shivered slightly with the cold. Noticing, Gerald said, 'Oh, would you like my coat?'

Miriam turned to him and said, 'My goodness. Quite simply, you are perfect!' she looked down and up at him again before saying, 'Not your coat. Just this. . .' and suddenly she leant forward and kissed him.

Gerald was so stunned, that for a moment he just sat there. But he quickly came to his senses. This woman didn't feel, smell, or taste like his beloved. Everything felt alien and wrong. This wasn't him and this wasn't who he was. He loved his wife and family. What was this woman doing?

Gerald hastily pushed Miriam back and wiping his lips with the back of his hand he said, 'I'm sorry, you have completely the wrong idea. I love my wife.'

Miriam sat back as if she'd been stung. She wasn't used to being rejected. 'Oh.' she said. 'I see. Sorry. Mis-read the signs.'

Gerald cleared his throat and replied, 'No. No problem. Flattered and all that. Just, I don't. Well, anyway. Not me.'

'Yes, obviously.' Miriam frostily replied and turned to her phone.

Ten minutes later the taxi driver returned to a distinctly chilled atmosphere. Brushing the snow off his knees he tried to say something cheerful, didn't get much of a response, indicated out of the pull-in and continued their journey to Manchester. Gerald and Miriam didn't talk, and the rest of the journey passed without event, except when Miriam dropped her phone on the floor and scrabbled about in the darkness trying to find it. When Gerald finally found the button for his torch on his phone, he found her looking up angrily at him and he wished he hadn't put it on at all.

The taxi pulled up along Gerald's street. Home was picked out by multicoloured, twinkling, fairy lights on the tree in the front garden and racing, icicle lights along the gutters. It was nearly six a.m. and still dark inside and out. Everybody was safely asleep waiting for Christmas Eve. Gerald knew his daughters and his wife would be glad that he was finally home. In fact, they'd probably be up in an hour or two.

Gerald insisted on paying for the entire fare, even though Miriam looked like she'd eaten a lemon at the gesture. Despite this, Gerald genuinely wished her, 'Happy Christmas' and gave a generous tip to the driver (which he was very happy about). Gerald then waved them goodbye until they were out of sight at the end of his road and turned gratefully for home.

❊ ❊ ❊

The familiar red brick and white plaster house welcomed him in. The entrance arch embraced him like a warm pair of arms. His wife had thoughtfully added little, lit, hanging stars in the porch. The fir tree in the front garden shone its multicoloured lights on a very tired and relieved Gerald as he walked up the path.

Gerald quietly opened the front door, pushed in his briefcase and suitcase, diligently took off his shoes and softly padded inside, slowly and carefully closing the door behind him. He took off his coat and quietly placed it on the coat stand. The house was silent apart from his dog, Old Faithful, who rushed up to Gerald from his basket, licking and wagging his tail in equal measure.

'Shh, old friend.' Gerald said, 'Quiet now. Let's get some treats from the kitchen, shall we?' Obediently the dog followed Gerald through.

From the hall lamp, Gerald could just make out six-fifteen on the kitchen clock. If he was lucky, he might get a few hours' sleep. He rubbed his eyes and went to the cupboard to grab some dog biscuits. Then he opened the fridge for a glass of milk. He nearly jumped out of his skin when he closed the fridge door to find his wife standing behind it.

Her platinum blonde hair waved around her head, and her fluffy, cream, cashmere pyjama set clung to every curve. Without words, Gerald dropped the milk on the counter and they clung to each other. Not an inch of light between their bodies.

She said, 'I've missed you.'

Tenderly he kissed the top of her head saying, 'I've missed you too my love. Cutting it a bit fine this year. I don't think I want to do that again.'

She buried her head into his chest and shook it

sadly, "No".

Gently, he reached down to her face, and lifting her chin, softly kissed her. Drawing back slightly, he looked down into her eyes by the dim light from the hall lamp and said, 'Home.' Before lightly kissing her again. He never grew tired of her kisses. This was all he ever wanted. There was nowhere else he wanted to be.

Eventually, Gerald drew back and said, 'I was going to keep this for tomorrow. But, somehow, I think the right moment is now.'

His wife looked confused as he led her by the hand through into the hall and knelt by his briefcase. Glancing up and smiling at her, he unzipped it and plunged his hand inside. He scrabbled around a bit, and looking confused dug a bit deeper. Then he took his laptop out and switching on the bottom hall light, began to take the contents of his briefcase out. The necklace wasn't there.

With a sinking feeling, Gerald thought back to the taxi and the dropped phone. The look Miriam had given him. He couldn't believe it. There was no other explanation. But, could she really have done something so selfish?

Gulping, Gerald stood up slowly and said, 'I'm so sorry darling, there looks to have been some mix-up. I've got you a present, but I must have left it in Munich. I'll contact the shop this morning and see if they can find a. . .'

Tap. Tap. Tap.

There was a very soft knock at the door. Gerald stopped mid-sentence and motioning his wife back into the hall behind him, he put his eye to the viewer, to see who was there. With a puzzled brow, he carefully undid the locks and quietly pulled back the door.

A forlorn-looking Miriam stood on the doorstep. The taxi driver had pulled up on the street outside, waiting. Reaching out her hand, Miriam deposited a small red box into Gerald's hand. 'Happy Christmas to you both.' she said. And giving a tight smile, turned for the taxi.

'Miriam,' Gerald called after her.

Miriam turned in the lifting darkness of a snowy Christmas Eve.

'Thank you, Miriam, Happy Christmas to you too.' Gerald said and smiled a genuine, kind smile. He was so glad to have the precious gift back.

Smiling again, properly this time, she waved her hand and headed straight back to the taxi. She was gone.

Gerald turned back to the glaring eyes of his wife. 'Who was that?' she demanded.

'Just a friend.' Gerald said warmly. 'And she has delivered this. Your present. I thought I'd forgotten it or lost it. But here it is after all.'

His wife's cross face softened as she accepted the small red box.

'Go on.' Gerald encouraged, 'Open it.'

Cautiously, his wife lifted the lid. Then immediately clamped her hand over her mouth. Tears sprang to her eyes as she stuttered, 'But. . . How did you? It's. . . ?' Her words escaped her.

Gerald's heart swelled. It was the perfect Christmas present.

Thank you for reading:

Three Christmas Presents
and other short stories

I would be so grateful if you would give me a review. I have some other book suggestions below, and at the end of this book an extract from **Màiri**, a Scottish romance novel.

Happy Christmas! HL x

You may be excited to read from the Christmas Collection (on Amazon):

**The Adventure of the Christmas Cracker
Snow Angels**

Also:

**I Don't Do Affairs
I Won't Let You In
I Can't Marry You
Rich Man
Poor Man**

Thief
Màiri
Isla
Dating Advice for Men

Coming in 2026:

Hiding a Thief
Catching a Thief
Loving a Thief
Meridah
The Secrets of Dating

and

Miss Scarlett Andrews Investigates
(Murder Mysteries)

MÀIRI CHAPTER 1

Màiri turned her moss-green eyes to look out at the cool, grey-blue, autumn waters, which were swirling beside the golden sands of Cruden Bay. The salty air filled her nose, and above her, seagulls were buffeted and bounced by the breeze. On the horizon, far away, she could see a trawler ship slowly passing through the rough waves. Her eyes watched it lurch through the water until it was a tiny dot on the horizon.

Màiri swept a light-blond strand of hair back from her pale, heart-shaped face. She sighed. The sound was lost to the wind. Worry lines pinched her forehead and dragged down at her jowls. She let them stay.

She looked down at her faithful friend and companion, Fudge, as the wind played with his soft curls of snowy-white hair and his little legs shook with the cold. He had stuck loyally by her side for the last five years. In many ways, she was closer to Fudge, her West Highland terrier, than she was to her family. She loved these quiet walks with him; stolen moments of peace. He was a dear little thing.

Fudge sat obediently at Màiri's feet and watched her gaze as she looked out again at the cool, grey-blue waters. Her heart thought, "I wonder if he is out there now, on a trawler, bringing in the nets? . . I wonder if he died? But they'll never tell me, and I can't ask. I wonder what would have happened if. . ." her eyebrows pulled together sharply.

She shook her head and she gulped back at the tears that were stinging her eyes. Pulling in a last deep breath of the cooling autumn air, she turned her face from the sea.

Once again, the breeze played with strands of her hair that had fallen loose from her bun. It was as if the wind was taunting her and tugging at her emotions, as if it wanted her to cry.

Màiri made a low whistle for Fudge to follow her along the beach.

As if allowing herself one last guilty thought, Màiri let her eyes wander and look over at the sand dunes. A warm, deep glow, not forgotten, filled her body. It may have been more than twenty years ago, but here, in this little, lost, golden-sand bay, omitted by tourists and busy locals, was the place of her greatest happiness. They couldn't take that away from her because only two people knew. And it was likely only one of them was alive to remember.

Beating down her thumping heart, Màiri pulled in a deep breath, looked away from the dunes and gently released the memory to the breeze. She pulled her old, puffy, khaki coat tighter around her body, as dog and owner walked quietly along the beautiful, sweeping sands of Cruden Bay, in the cool, swirling, salty air of a quiet afternoon.

❋ ❋ ❋

Fudge liked to sit right up front in the passenger seat and *woof* and *yap* at the passers-by.

As Màiri manoeuvred her old, grey, Volvo hatchback out from the parking space near the small harbour and headed towards the road, a sleek, black Ferrari with tinted windows smoothly pulled past her, along the road through the village.

Màiri clutched at her heart.

Suddenly, she worried she was going to have a panic attack – just like she used to. She shivered violently and took a deep breath. A cold chill flashed through her spine, her chest clenched painfully, and her breath caught in her throat.

Stopping the car sharply, Màiri caged her heart with rigid hands. Fudge stumbled on his passenger seat, and they watched the black Ferrari slowly slide along the main street and pull into the local council car park.

Màiri gasped for oxygen and sucked in her breath, refilling her body. Slowly, she regained her composure and the pain subsided.

She looked up from under her heavy eyes. Whose car was it? Cruden Bay was one of her favourite spots to walk Fudge; it was where her family had their holiday home. She hadn't seen a car like that around here before. Ever.

She shook her head, trying to let her troubled thoughts slide. Màiri put her car into gear and manoeuvred the large hatchback out of the small fishing village and north, up the road, past the council car park, past the sleek black car, towards the fishing port of Peterhead; the most significant fishing harbour in Scotland.

* * *

Màiri turned the steering wheel. She drove down into the wide bay, into Peterhead, through the houses, towards her family's beautiful, enormous Victorian villa. Her eyes wandered along the view of the bay before her.

She drove along the old streets with high pink-granite walls, guarded by high, twisted iron gates. Behind each wall lay a beautiful Victorian villa, built for the wealthy fishing families when Peter-head had been at the height of its fortunes.

Pulling through a pair of large, pink, Peterhead granite gate posts and onto a crunchy gravel drive, Màiri pulled past her parents' large house, which was made of thick granite walls, tall windows, high window gables, and carved, white-painted wood fascias. A house to last, a house to hold testament to its wealth. She steered the car slowly around the back, towards the garages. Tucking her battered Volvo neatly inside an open garage, she let Fudge out.

Fudge bounded into the enormous back garden, which was enclosed on all sides by the high granite walls. It was mainly left to lawn, with a few abandoned, leggy shrubs scattered about. Fudge sniffed and ran, hopped and bounced; a fluffy white dot in the rarely-cut grass. He was desperate to explore and sniff out any cats who might have dared to cross onto their land since he'd left just a few hours earlier.

Slowly, Màiri locked her car and crunched out onto the gravel. She looked up. Above her head, seagulls screamed and cried. She could smell the fish from the harbour even this far into town. Turning towards the house, her eyebrows rose. Her father's Porsche was parked messily around the side of the garages. Her eyebrows pulled together and her mouth tightened. He always parked in the garage and was never home this early. Her father was as predictable as a clock.

Ian Esson loved to work because he loved the money, power and control it gave him, and it was rare for him to be back before dinner most evenings. Màiri had once wondered if he kept another woman, but he was too busy for that. His business, "Esson Fisheries", was the largest private fishing company in the port of Peterhead. He owned eight trawler ships and nineteen smaller fishing boats, alongside several large warehouses and two fish shops; one here in Peterhead and one in Aberdeen, where her sister Lynne and brother-in-law Steve lived and worked. Ian was always busy, but even more so now that some of the trawlers and nets were getting repaired, ready for the start of the autumn fishing season for Haddock. There was work to do and Ian was the man to do it.

Màiri whistled to Fudge to come inside. She made her way past the enormous Victorian conservatory, which was flaking white paint like dandruff. Opening the old, thick, cracked-black-gloss-painted oak back door, Màiri held it for Fudge as he bounded in before her. She softly commanded him to wait, took off her leather ankle boots and reached up for his towel from the dark, carved-wood, Victorian coat rack, and started gently drying his little paws.

Fudge sniffed up at Màiri's face in familiarity; it was almost as if he was giving her a little reassuring kiss on her nose. Telling her that everything was going to be okay.

Looking into his large, dark, bulging eyes, Màiri affectionately tickled his head and tugged his little ears, saying in her soft Scottish accent, 'Darling little one. Mummy loves you very much. You're a good boy.'

Fudge made a small *woof* and bounded off, deeper into the house.

Màiri slowly took off her thick, padded coat and hung it on the rack. Inside the house, possibly from the drawing room at the front, she heard raised voices, and her father shout in his deep, thick, Peterhead accent:

'It's a monstrosity! He must have paid a backhander to the council to get *that* approved. A disgusting display of wealth, flashing his cash around. It's common. I cannae believe that the planning has got this far. I will talk to Robbie MacBride myself this evening. I won't have that jumped-up little *loon* throwing his money around here. I've put him in his place once and I'll do it again!' His 'rs' rolled heavily like the sound of thunder.

Màiri gave an involuntary shiver; she could hear the menace in her father's voice and she knew the consequences of it. She could just about make out the soft, sweet, soothing Scottish tones of her mother's voice, too quiet to hear the actual words, but the intention was clear; she was trying to pacify her angry husband.

In contrast, Màiri could also hear her mother's sister, Màiri's Aunt Anne, in her strong Scottish accent echoing back Màiri's father's indignation to him: 'I completely agree! Such a vulgar display of wealth is disgusting. And we all know it's *not* through hard work. Well, Ian, you know what they say, easy come, easy go. We will have the last laugh as we watch him fall flat on his face. Again. We'll watch him go.'

Once again, Màiri could hear the soft, sweet tones of her mother trying to calm the agitated adults, but her voice was overpowered by her husband replying, 'Aye, you're right there, Anne. And when the day comes, which will not be so far away, I will celebrate his demise with a dram of my thirty-year-old special Lochnagar single malt. Nothing will give me greater pleasure than to open *that* bottle to toast to his failure. It is a sweet irony. I'll be drinking something that is his complete opposite in every way; classy and refined!'

Fudge dashed into the drawing room, and Màiri could hear her mother loudly exclaim, 'Oh, little Fudge! You're all sandy and damp! Where is Màiri?'

Màiri wasn't sure, but she thought she heard her aunt say, "*Shh.*"

Uncertainly, Màiri walked through the grand hallway and gingerly poked her head around the drawing room door. Hesitantly, she slowly walked into the enormous room.

The room would have been the height of fashion and taste, thirty years ago. It had a garish red-and-brown patterned, thick wool carpet, which was decidedly thin along the threshold into the drawing room and around the massive, carved, pink-granite fireplace, which was a true testament to the craft of the Victorians. The open fire had been replaced years ago by a smaller, practical stove and tiled in with beige, iridescent, square tiles; in complete contrast to the heavy, dark-wood, Victorian furniture; and thick, red, velvet curtains. The room was about four metres square, and the tall, wide, bay window at the front looked out onto a relatively modest front garden.

The garden was separated from the streets of Peterhead by high, pink-granite walls that ran around from the front to the back and safely enclosed the property from less desirables. However, the large, black-gloss-painted but rusting in places, twisted iron gates lay open, and grass ensnared their base. It was as if someone had forgotten to close them long ago and then couldn't be bothered anymore. The opening led out to the road that ran through to the centre of town. The gates were never used (who would dare to cross *this* threshold uninvited?) and the pink Peterhead granite gravel tried to escape from the driveway onto the road, ready to be swept away by the industrious road sweepers.

The relatively modest area of lawn was parted from the main house by the large sweeping gravel drive as it crashed around the side of the house and swept through to the back, like the surge of the tide. A few large, leggy, unruly shrubs persisted in the front garden, not dissimilar to those at the back of the house, and they were clutching at the last of their leaves before the cold winter. There *were* a handful of impressively tall pine trees next to the front garden wall (where they would be seen) forever brooding, standing proud and looking down their noses at the passers-by outside the villa walls, but truth be told, they too should have been trimmed back years ago. Instead, they grew tall and mighty, too close to the enclosing high granite wall, which was starting to crack as they towered over it. Unaware, the dark-green pine trees loomed over the walls and gave snide hints to the passers-by of the mighty grandness of the property within, but failed to look behind, to see what it had become.

Inside the drawing room, in the centre of the room, hanging from the ceiling, was a beautiful cut-glass chandelier, held by a moulded ceiling rose with scrolls, grapes and delicate flowers. The cornicing around the room also had the same ornate moulding and was a reminder of the opulent wealth from another era, but the walls were magnolia with spots of damp, and the velvet furniture was threadbare in places; a dim memory of when they were new, and fashionable.

Màiri looked at the adults around her. Her father, Ian Esson, was pacing the room with his fists clenched. He was a huge man, standing at least six-foot-three and weighing possibly as much as sixteen stone. Màiri would never dare ask. His arms were thick and muscly, and his chest hearty and broad. Although he was over sixty now, he dyed his hair black, his skin was healthy and tanned, and his teeth glowed white. He liked to wear fine-cut suits and shirts over his thick, muscly torso. Today he wore some expensive designer jeans; a light-blue handmade shirt, open at the neck; and a thin, light-grey wool blazer. He wore a tan leather belt and tan Italian leather shoes. He was pacing through the room as he raked his hand through his hair, before clenching his fists again.

Ian looked over quickly as Màiri cautiously came further into the drawing room, and the irritation left his face as a neutral expression appeared. In his thick Peterhead accent, he said, 'I see you've come back from yer walk?'

Màiri nodded in deference, then looked over at her mother, who was sat on the end of an old velvet sofa near the stove. She was fussing with Fudge and looked similar to Màiri in almost every way, only twenty years older. Her face was lined and her features were delicate. She had the same fine, light-blonde hair, which fluffed and curled around her head and was kept artificially blonde by regular trips to the hairdresser. Just like Màiri, she had the same moss-green eyes and the same gentle nature; Margaret Esson was sweetly beautiful. She looked up from her soft seat on the sofa and asked Màiri, 'Did you have a nice walk, darling? Did you go to Cruden Bay?'

Màiri nodded, gulped, and said, 'Yes, I was hoping to see some seals but I couldn't see any today. The weather is fresh and fine though.'

Across the room, Màiri's Aunt Anne scoffed as she leant forward from her position on the other large sofa; her pinched nose and tightly held salt-and-pepper hair straining as she replied, 'Well, I'm glad at least one of us is calm and relaxed. I'll doubt you'll be so soon though, girl, when you hear the news. Nothing more than a testament to how low the council has stooped to take bribes. I'm quite sure they are desperate for money to line their pockets since your father has stopped being quite so generous.' And she shot Ian a significant look with her small, dark eyes.

Màiri raised her eyebrows at her aunt and turned to look at her father, whom she found had been watching her cautiously, as she asked, 'What is the news, Father?'

Ian Esson swallowed heavily and wrinkled his thick nose as he spat out, 'The council have approved a development. An enormous house! Some ridiculous glass and concrete monstrosity is going to be built to the south of the bay. On the site of one of our first warehouses, which you may remember we sold for development two years ago. Apparently, the whole area is to be "positively impacted" by this new building. And apparently, the house build is going to cost one million to build. At least! It's a disgusting waste of money.'

Her father started pacing again, and Màiri turned to look between her father and her aunt as she enquired, 'Who is it? Who's building this house?'

Màiri's aunt sharply replied, 'We have no idea, Màiri! But that's not the point. Clearly, there's been some backhanders at the council. No decent authority would allow planning for such a monstrosity. And on our land too!'

Màiri turned back to look at her father and found he was scowling at the floor, his clenched fists blanching of blood in his tight grip.

Trying to defuse the situation, Màiri said, 'I guess I'd better give Fudge a rubdown with a damp towel and try and brush the sand out of his hair.'

Màiri's aunt quickly added, 'I ask you to do that every time, girl. But you always forget. Sometimes I think you do it on purpose. I know we have a cleaner, but we do have to pay her. Something you seem to take for granted.'

Màiri gulped heavily and replied, 'Yes, Aunt, I'm sorry. He slipped out of my hands before I had a chance to wipe him down properly.'

She looked over at her mother, who was tickling little Fudge's ears and completely oblivious to her aunt's reprimands. All she could think about was removing herself from this angry, buzzy room and getting back to her quiet spot in the conservatory as soon as possible, so she could bury her head in a romance book and imagine herself away in her mind.